Roanne mumbl[...]
the whole thing [...] [...]
set off the other?"

"That would be bad," Nolan conceded. He dropped his phone in a pocket. "Hey. Come here.

He held out his arms and she all but threw herself into his embrace. Was she shaking? Maybe—but she thought he was, too.

"Thank God we have experts out there who know how to take care of bombs." Nolan's fervency sounded genuine. "I'm just glad it's not my job anymore."

Roanne held on tight, her voice muffled against Nolan's broad, solid chest. "That was...a really close call." She was afraid her teeth were actually chattering. What if she'd seen him die, and in what might be the most horrible way of all?

EXPLOSIVE THREAT

JANICE KAY JOHNSON

INTRIGUE

If you purchased this book without a cover you should be aware that this book is stolen property. It was reported as "unsold and destroyed" to the publisher, and neither the author nor the publisher has received any payment for this "stripped book."

ISBN-13: 978-1-335-69041-8

Explosive Threat

Copyright © 2025 by Janice Kay Johnson

All rights reserved. No part of this book may be used or reproduced in any manner whatsoever without written permission.

Without limiting the exclusive rights of any author, contributor or the publisher of this publication, any unauthorized use of this publication to train generative artificial intelligence (AI) technologies is expressly prohibited. Harlequin also exercises their rights under Article 4(3) of the Digital Single Market Directive 2019/790 and expressly reserves this publication from the text and data mining exception.

This is a work of fiction. Names, characters, places and incidents are either the product of the author's imagination or are used fictitiously. Any resemblance to actual persons, living or dead, businesses, companies, events or locales is entirely coincidental.

For questions and comments about the quality of this book, please contact us at CustomerService@Harlequin.com.

TM and ® are trademarks of Harlequin Enterprises ULC.

 Harlequin Enterprises ULC
22 Adelaide St. West, 41st Floor
Toronto, Ontario M5H 4E3, Canada
www.Harlequin.com

HarperCollins Publishers
Macken House, 39/40 Mayor Street Upper,
Dublin 1, D01 C9W8, Ireland
www.HarperCollins.com

Printed in Lithuania

An author of more than ninety books for children and adults with more than seventy-five for Harlequin, **Janice Kay Johnson** writes about love and family, and pens books of gripping romantic suspense. A *USA TODAY* bestselling author and an eight-time finalist for the Romance Writers of America RITA® Award, she won a RITA® Award in 2008. A former librarian, Janice raised two daughters in a small town north of Seattle, Washington.

Books by Janice Kay Johnson

Harlequin Intrigue

Hide the Child
Trusting the Sheriff
Within Range
Brace for Impact
The Hunting Season
The Last Resort
Cold Case Flashbacks
Dead in the Water
Mustang Creek Manhunt
Crime Scene Connection
High Mountain Terror
The Sheriff's to Protect
Crash Landing
Black Widow
Wilderness Hostage
Storing Secrets
Explosive Threat

Visit the Author Profile page at Harlequin.com.

CAST OF CHARACTERS

Roanne Engle—A detective who happens to be in the right place to dispose of the first bomb, she continues, despite injuries, to join forces with FBI Agent Cantrell to find the bomb maker before more lethal explosions threaten the citizens she protects.

Nolan Cantrell—Supervisory FBI Agent Cantrell is a natural for this hunt after his time spent defusing IEDs in the military. He feels as if he's playing catch-up as other homemade bombs kill and injure the citizens of a usually peaceful town. Falling in love with the detective? A distraction he should be able to resist.

Charles Anderson—Only a miracle in the person of Detective Engle saves Superior Court Judge Anderson from a package bomb left on his desk.

Dwayne Knepper aka Theodoros—Cult leader Theodoros is imprisoned after beating a child to death. But is he somehow controlling his followers from prison?

Andy Spooner—Trying to stay faithful to his leader, Andy both protects the remnants of the cult and feels shamed when he fails.

Blaine Weightman—Businessman Blaine sells and repairs office machinery. His presence in the courtroom the day the first bomb detonates places him under suspicion.

Chapter One

Detective Roanne Engle had almost reached her city-issued car when she decided she really needed a restroom. Mostly, it would be preventative. Her next stop was to interview a former county councilman who had been accused of sexual assault by a staff member. He wasn't likely to receive her visit well. She certainly couldn't ask to use his bathroom. She could have met with him much more conveniently this afternoon in his insurance office, but he'd insisted she come out to his house sometime after 5:30. Roanne didn't have grounds yet to justify being more forceful with an important man in the county.

Unfortunately, she also felt a little queasy. A flu had been going around, mowing down all ranks in the Rosendaal Police Department. With a little luck, she was reacting to the heaping pile of french fries she'd succumbed to at lunch. Either way...

She was closer to the handsome, traditional courthouse than to the front entrance of the more modern wing that housed the prosecutor's office she'd just come from. At this time of day, the courthouse would be mostly deserted.

Fine. The guards all knew her and would wave her in, no problem. A small city north of Seattle, Washington, Rosendaal still hadn't modernized to screen entrants with an X-ray machine and metal-detection equipment. No, the city had never had a shoot-out in a courtroom, but in Roanne's opinion, it would happen sooner or later. Better to prepare than pay the consequences.

Right now, though, she *really* needed that bathroom.

She took the marble steps two at a time, then waved at the guards and started down the nearest hallway before seeing the Out of Service sandwich board in front of the women's restroom.

Upstairs, then.

She'd just made it to the second story and started toward the restroom sign when an imperative voice called to her.

"Roanne? Is that you?"

Wonderful. She'd been dodging Judge Charles Anderson lately because she'd appeared as a witness in his courtroom several times in the past six months. It was one thing to be his pal when he was one of the guests at her father's house. Being seen cozying up to a state superior court judge, and in the courthouse no less, wasn't a good idea for a cop, especially not a Major Crimes detective.

Still, she could hardly ignore him. The late-afternoon hour meant most offices were deserted and the hall was quiet. Roanne took the few steps to his office, closest to the grand staircase, and stopped in his open doorway. "Judge."

"Trying to tiptoe by, were you?"

A handsome man in his late fifties—she'd seen him blow out the forest of candles on his cake at his last birthday party—Judge Anderson had deep-cut lines that betrayed his willingness to smile...and to silence someone in court with a withering look or sharp edge of his tongue.

She propped a shoulder on his doorjamb. She wasn't

quite squirming but getting close. "Just making sure nobody questions my next appearance in your courtroom."

In his deep, rumbling voice, he said, "Bah! Let them question. Can't change the fact that I've known you since you were in diapers."

It was true. He and her father had been roommates at the University of Washington forty years ago and had stayed close ever since.

Right now, the judge was wielding a letter opener. As she watched, he sliced the tops of several envelopes, barely glancing before tossing them aside. Apparently he had no trouble multitasking.

"What brought you here today?" he asked.

She wrinkled her nose. "Restroom downstairs is out of order. I figured I could just run up here and use this one."

He laughed heartily, reaching for what appeared to be a package that was next in his heap of mail. He said something else, but her attention had snagged on the odd package. A subliminal feeling sparked alarm, and she straightened. No, they'd never had a bombing in Rosendaal, either, but the package looked *wrong*.

The effect of sloppy brown-paper wrapping coupled with big, block-like letters formed with a black marker was almost childlike. A grandkid could have sent this… but to him at work?

Roanne acted without thinking. She leaped across the office just as Judge Anderson started to slice the paper with that letter opener. Was that the end of a wire visible beneath a strip of packing tape?

She snatched it from him, raced back to the hall and, seeing nobody, threw the package in an arc toward the open space at the top of the staircase. Please God no one was mounting the stairs. If she were overreacting…

The fiery burst of light blinded her as a boom assaulted her eardrums and she was flung from her feet. Even with her arms wrapped around her head, she felt the crack as her skull struck marble. Pain stung her body, and darkness swallowed her.

NOLAN CANTRELL WOULD have enjoyed the long weekend away from work more if he hadn't felt the tension between his sister and his brother-in-law. It wasn't overt enough that he'd pushed Ellen for an explanation; the couple of times he'd tiptoed that direction, she'd turned a defiant look on him that told him she had no intention of opening up to him.

Nolan wanted to believe he'd just visited at an off time. It would be a rare couple's relationship that consistently stayed sunshine and roses. What he was seeing was mere irritation, the remnants of a squabble. In his line of work, though, he'd become sensitive to nuances. This felt as if a trip wire was stretched so tight between them, a touch would set it off.

Even behind the wheel of his car, he winced at the analogy. He'd seen the gory results of a bomb triggered by a trip wire. This wasn't anything like that.

He also acknowledged that he'd never liked Brian Thurman all that much. He'd tried. Ellen insisted Nolan and Brian had a lot in common, both being law enforcement officers. He'd tried to explain that was like saying plumbers were all alike, or doctors. She didn't get it. A deputy in a rural Washington state county—Grant County—Brian had the swagger and arrogance Nolan saw too often.

There wasn't a thing he could do but be prepared to offer his support when his sister's marriage imploded. He wasn't cut out to offer anything constructive anyway. It wasn't like *he'd* been able to sustain a relationship. Or, for that matter, been sure he wanted one.

Growing up seeing his father's dominance and his mother's meekness probably had something to do with that. He had no doubt Ellen had replicated what she'd seen growing up at home when she chose a blusterer who frequently talked right over her as if nothing she had to say was worth hearing.

He felt mostly relief as he steered west on a minor highway. This part of the state usually was a monotonous brown, but spring had spread a carpet of green. Unfortunately, there was no direct route to Seattle; a sign told him he was approaching Wenatchee, where he intended to grab a bite to eat, then hop on the major highway that would take him over Stevens Pass to the west side of the mountains. The lifts at the ski resort would be long-closed for the season. He gave passing thought to the last time he'd skied and couldn't remember.

Not a good sign. His preoccupation with his job left him little time for anything else, as several women he'd dated had pointed out.

As always, he shoved the thought aside.

His phone rang and he answered with "Cantrell."

"Nolan, I can't remember where you are. Aren't you due back to work in the morning?"

"I am. I just reached Wenatchee."

"That's good news." Rare relief sounded in FBI Special Agent in Charge Todd Simmons's voice. "You familiar with Rosendaal? It seems to be up Skagit County way."

"Vaguely," he said. He pictured vast fields of tulips and daffodils, the cultivation of which the area was known for. Rosendaal surely had been named by Dutch settlers. Not a gardener, he didn't think he'd ever had occasion to get off I-5 to look for the town before.

"A package bomb addressed to a state superior court judge just went off in the courthouse."

Nolan's jaw tightened. "Did it kill him?"

"No. From what I'm told, a police officer had stopped by his office and, according to him, leaped to grab the package just as he sliced into it with his letter opener. She threw it out into the deserted hall, where it went off. She was injured. If she's regained consciousness yet, I haven't heard. Right now, that's about all I *have* heard. I want you to take this one."

Nolan had taken an exit and pulled into the parking lot of a sandwich shop. "Okay. Text me names and anything else you learn. I'm still several hours away. I assume you've made contact with someone at the ATF?"

"Yes, and they expect to have an NRT in place tomorrow sometime." The Bureau of Alcohol, Tobacco, Firearms and Explosives had rapid-response teams based in strategic parts of the country. In a case like this, the FBI was likely to head the investigation side, while the members of the National Response Team—certified explosive specialists, bomb technicians, forensic chemists and just about everything else required—would crawl over the scene like ants at a picnic, analyzing the bomb by locating the tiniest possible components and putting them together like a jigsaw puzzle while also advising every other law enforcement agency descending on the rural city on what those components had to say about the bomb maker's possible age, sophistication and, certainly, experience. The unit's skills were invaluable.

Simmons continued as if he'd read Nolan's mind. "I'm not going all in yet. One bomb, didn't kill anybody, probably turn out to be crude. It could even be personal to the judge or have been aimed at an assistant who usually opens his mail. Now, if there's a repetition..."

He didn't have to finish his sentence. Unlike serial arsonists, serial bombers were rare, especially in a nice town surrounded by glorious swaths of blooming tulips. Instructions for building pipe bombs and the like were easily found on the internet. An angry fifteen-year-old could probably build one.

However... a judge had been targeted and the bomb somehow delivered to him *inside* a courthouse. Federal investigators had no choice but to jump in.

"I don't suppose you know whether the package came through the mail?" Nolan asked.

"No idea. The judge is distraught, but he said he hardly glanced at the package while he was talking to the detective. The wrapping is probably shredded and burned. With luck, the cop will have noticed."

"Okay. I'm grabbing a sandwich to eat on my way and will head directly to Rosendaal. Ah..."

"Expect me to be your concierge, do you?"

Nolan smiled but didn't answer.

"I'll get my assistant to make reservations and text that info, too. Keep in touch."

"Will do," Nolan agreed, ending the call.

No more than fifteen minutes later, sandwich in hand, he was back on the road. In one way, his mood had improved; he must've been a hunter by nature, because he thrived in his job. He was already turning over the little he knew in his head, anticipating learning more. He was a natural to head this investigation because he was one of the few current agents in the Seattle FBI office who had any background with bombs. He'd done a number of years in the military as an explosive ordnance disposal technician. When he chose not to re-up, a recruiter from the ATF had been waiting with a job offer he had immediately declined. The members of the rapid-response teams were almost entirely made up of people like him who'd learned the trade courtesy of the US Army or another branch of the military.

Yeah, he knew IEDs, but he still came awake from a nightmare every month or so reliving his experiences. *Flashback* might've been a better word. Despite his confidence and experience and faith in his teammates and the trained dogs that assisted them, he'd developed a phobia that last year. Every time he approached an explosive device he thought, *This might be the one.* He *knew* he wouldn't survive to retire, to go home again.

And yet he had. So now he had a familiar crawling sensation up his spine, ending with the prickle of the close-cropped hair on the back of his neck.

He would be unlikely to be the one laying hands on future devices, assuming there were any. But if worse came to worse…he was damn good at defusing them.

What he needed first was to talk to the cop who'd had a sharp enough eye to recognize something that didn't belong and reactions quick enough to save at least one life while risking her own.

Unless, of course, she'd planted the bomb to make herself appear a heroine. Unlikely, but something he'd have to rule out.

His phone had been dinging with incoming texts. Shortly after the exit, he pulled off the road to glance at them and saw her name: Detective Roanne Engle, currently to be found in the small community hospital.

He'd go there first.

ROANNE EMERGED FROM darkness to a massive headache. She lay still, not sure she wanted to open her eyes. She thought there was a *beep, beep, beep* coming from nearby but might've been imagining things. Her ears felt as if they'd been stuffed with wax. What if she *couldn't* open her eyes?

She hurt other places, too. Shoulder, hip, one wrist that seemed to be encased in wrappings or a cast.

"Roanne," said a quiet and familiar voice. "Your breathing has changed. Are you back with us?"

Her father. For him, she had to *try*.

Somehow she pried open eyelids that had to weigh ten pounds each. Her eyes felt gritty, and her reward was a blurry scene that was too bright. Her father gradually came into focus.

He didn't look like himself. Wrinkles she hadn't known were there had become crevasses.

"Dad?" she said uncertainly.

"Oh, thank God!" He seized one of her hands and squeezed. "You scared the daylights out of me!"

Her, too. Except she didn't remember what she'd done to deserve taking a pounding. Had she been beaten up? No, she'd had to pee—she did remember that much—and been sick to her stomach besides. In fact, it chose to lurch now. Her father read her well enough to whisk a basin at hand for her to bring up a thin stream of bile. He helped her rinse her mouth afterward, too.

"How long have I been out?" she mumbled. "Is this the same day?"

"Yes. It's about nine o'clock in the evening."

Evening. Her brain struggled to assemble the facts.

"Bomb." It came to her in living color, and she struggled to sit up. "Uncle Charles?" She'd called the judge that since her earliest childhood years, except not in public. Not once she'd signed on with the Rosendaal Police Department anyway.

"He's fine." Her dad's hand gently pressed her back to her pillow. "Thanks to you. I think he's going to write his boys out of his will and leave everything to you."

Roanne chuckled weakly, undoubtedly what he'd intended.

"Do you remember what happened, then?"

She started to nod before cringing and squeezing her eyes shut. *Don't move head.* Check. "Yes."

"There's already an FBI agent here, sitting in the waiting room hoping to be able to talk to you. I can tell him he has to wait until tomorrow—"

"No. It was so close. If I hadn't gone upstairs to use the ladies room, if I'd hesitated, Uncle Charles would have been killed. Wouldn't he?"

Her father's usually genial face appeared even grimmer. "From what I hear...yes."

"Send him in. I can tell him..." Well, she wasn't sure what. She'd acted on instinct. If she'd paused to think, she felt sure she would have convinced herself there was a nice present for the judge inside that package and that she'd break it by tossing it down the hall.

"Okay." Her dad bent over, kissed her forehead and said, "I'm proud of you. But don't do it again."

She thought she was smiling. Her eyes sank closed again as she heard the curtain rattle. *Beep, beep, beep.* She was the one being monitored.

Another faint rattle. She didn't hear so much as a footstep, but she could feel a presence. She fluttered her lashes and finally opened her eyes again.

The man standing beside her bed came into instant

focus in a way her father hadn't. He wasn't linebacker big, but he would have several inches on her father, who wasn't a short man. Broad shoulders, lean muscles like a basketball player rather than a weightlifter. His hair was dark, ruffled as if he hadn't combed it in the last day, and his eyes were a startling blue.

"Hello," she croaked.

He smiled, his grave expression surrendering to a warm flicker. "Detective Engle, I'm told."

"Yes."

"I'm FBI Special Agent Nolan Cantrell. I'm here ahead of the hordes that will probably follow me."

She looked at him in perplexity. "Hordes?"

"Someone tried to kill a judge in the courthouse with a bomb. That tends to get the attention of federal agencies. The Bureau of Alcohol, Tobacco, Firearms and Explosives has a team of experts on the way, but they're coming from Southern California, so we won't see them until tomorrow."

"Oh." This was a big deal. If she'd had time to think about it, she'd have known this wasn't an investigation to be left in the hands of a smallish city police department. "You're from the Seattle office?"

"I am, although I was heading toward Stevens Pass after a visit with family in Moses Lake. When I reached Everett, I turned north on I-5 instead of south."

"Have you...been to the courthouse?"

"No, we have it roped off until the NRT—the rapid-response team—gets here. They'll be hunting for every shred that will tell them what they need to know about the bomb. How skilled was the bomber? Did he have experience, or was this a crude first attempt that surprised even him by working?" Special Agent Cantrell said. "The judge ran out after the bomb went off, but he was focused on you and getting medics there. I gather he saw light flash beyond his office door and heard the boom, but he didn't actually see the detonation."

"Oh. I wish I hadn't."

"You mind if I pull up a chair?"

So this wasn't going to be a fleeting visit. Roanne felt something that surprised her: relief because she mostly could hand this over to him.

"Of course not."

The chair scraped across the vinyl floor. He settled his long body into it, bringing that intent gaze to a level that required her to turn her head slightly.

"Do you know anything about IEDs?" she asked.

"As it happens, I do." He hesitated. "I was a bomb-disposal expert in the army. I've only had a few occasions to deal with bombers since, though."

She would have nodded, except that wouldn't be a good idea. "What can I tell you?"

Predictably, he wanted to know what had caught her attention about that particular package and if anyone had threatened the judge.

"No one that I know of," she responded. "Honestly, I was trying to dodge him and use the restroom down the hall, but he heard me. He's a good friend of my father's. I've known Judge Anderson my entire life."

Nobody had ever looked at her with such intensity. He hardly blinked as he waited.

So she tried to put into words what hadn't exactly been a reasoned suspicion and clear-headed decision. "He wasn't paying any attention, just slitting his mail open while he talked to me. The package just looked *wrong*. Poorly wrapped, strange big block letters addressing it, and… I can't swear to this, but I thought I saw the end of a wire under the clear packing tape. I think it was that. It would have been embarrassing if it was a gift, but—"

"Sometimes you can't afford to pause. At worst, you'd have broken a nice mug somebody bought him."

"It didn't seem…quite big enough to have a mug in it, but…you're right, of course."

"Could you tell if it came through the US Postal Service?"

She stared at him, thinking. "I'm not sure, but I don't think so. That may have also been part of what set me off. How *did* it get in the pile of legitimate mail?"

"That," he said, "is an excellent question, Detective. One we'll be asking."

Chapter Two

He needed to learn a lot more about Roanne Engle, and intended to do so, but his first impressions had almost succeeded in squelching Nolan's brief speculation that this could have been a stunt. Both looking as if they'd seen hell on earth, two older men sat side by side in the waiting room. Nolan liked what he saw of them.

The judge, appearing considerably older than he probably was, stayed with Nolan while her father was permitted back in her room. Anderson seemed willing to talk about the young woman who'd saved his life today.

"Only child now," he said. "Her older brother was killed, oh, about ten years ago in a head-on accident. The other driver was drunk as a skunk and walked away."

"I assume he wasn't allowed to keep walking."

"No, but he didn't serve the time he deserved—that's for damn sure."

"He didn't come before you in court?"

"The accident happened down in King County. If it had been local I wouldn't have been able to preside, given that I loved those two. Roanne's father and I have been good friends since we roomed together in college. He became a CPA, and I went to law school. Didn't see as much of each other for a few years, but Rosendaal was his home town, and I decided to set up practice here, too.

"My wife and I have two boys, a little older than Phil's two," he continued. "Erik is an attorney now at a high-powered practice in Seattle, and my other boy drives trucks. He's diagnosed as having autism spectrum disorder. Good kid, but likes solitude. He's actually married now and has a baby girl." Judge Anderson's voice shook. "Roanne...well, I couldn't love that girl any more if she were my own."

Nolan kept him talking, both because he wanted to learn as much background as possible and because he sensed the judge needed to think back over the years. Even knowing as he now did that Roanne had regained consciousness, he was scared. Nolan didn't blame him. From what he'd been told, if the bomb had exploded even a second or two sooner, if her reaction time hadn't been so extraordinary, Detective Roanne Engle likely would have been killed. Actually, depending on how far away she'd been from his desk, she'd have had a good chance of dying anyway if she hadn't noticed the package the judge had been in the act of opening.

He tried to steer Judge Anderson to his recent trials, wanting to know if any had been particularly contentious. The judge didn't seem to understand and rambled instead.

The detective's father reappeared, allowing the judge to go in to see the young woman who'd saved his life. He didn't stay long.

"I think she needs to sleep," he said to her father. "If you're planning to stay the night—"

"Of course I am."

Nolan interjected, "May I suggest you both go home and try to rest? She doesn't need you right now, but she may tomorrow. I plan to stay for a while. If she gets distressed, I'll call you."

It took a good five minutes for the two older men to be persuaded, but at length they left, shuffling as if they were in their eighties. He felt empathy but had hopes Detective Engle would have wakeful periods tonight and might appreciate a sympathetic ear.

The nurse assigned to the detective was doubtful about letting him sit at the bedside but finally acceded as long as he promised not to wake up Detective Engle.

He had caught up on his sleep during the four days at his sister's, and this wouldn't be the first time he'd drifted in and out at a hospital bedside. When he'd first arrived in town, he had checked into the motel where his Special Agent in Charge's assistant had reserved a room, raised his brows at the plain, clean space—not much else could be said for it—and left his duffel there before going to the hospital. The bed hadn't looked that appealing anyway.

Now he sank low in a fairly comfortable chair and in the dim light from the hall watched the young woman toss and turn.

Was she always a restless sleeper? Or was she seeing that bomb explode over and over, imprinting the brilliant flash on the inside of her eyelids?

When she rolled away from him, the blankets down around her waist and her gown parting in back, he noticed a myriad of small dressings dotting a slim back. Bruising crept from beneath those dressings. He leaned forward but couldn't see well. Was that the result of nails or other shrapnel from the IED? Nobody had said.

His jaw muscles ached as he clenched his teeth. A crude bomb this might have been, but if the maker had progressed to wanting to inflict maximum injuries, that raised him a notch on Nolan's meter. She must have curled away to protect her head. He pictured it too clearly. If she hadn't, she'd have been pelted with sharp bits of metal in her face, potentially scarring or even blinding her.

This IED wasn't as simple or crude as Nolan had thought. Not that any budding bomb maker couldn't go online and read up on not only the basics but also the extras. All he'd have had to do was read about the Boston Marathon bombers.

She cried out and jerked upright, looking wildly around.

Nolan rose to his feet and reached for her hand. "Hey," he said gently. "You're in the hospital. You're safe here. I won't let anyone get close."

Eyes so dilated he wouldn't have known what color they were if he hadn't seen her earlier, she demanded sharply, "Who are you?"

"FBI Special Agent Nolan Cantrell." He kept his voice low and reassuring. "We talked earlier."

"Oh." She blinked a few times. "I thought Dad was staying."

"I sent him home to get some sleep. Told him I'd keep you company instead."

"Oh," she said again before letting her head fall forward. "I keep seeing—"

"I know." He rubbed his thumb on the back of her hand, feeling the fragility of her bones. "And you're not just seeing. You're hearing, and feeling the punch that threw you back."

"Yes. You've…?"

"I have." Once you'd experienced what she had today and come out alive on the other end, he wondered if anyone could forget.

"Thank you," she whispered.

Nolan helped her lie down, but it quickly became apparent that lying on her back wasn't comfortable. He adjusted pillows and covers so she could lie on her side, facing him. Then he took her hand again, even though he knew that wasn't a good idea.

Her fingers were long, slender and icy. He tried to warm the one he held, making sure her other hand was tucked beneath the covers. Which, he suspected, weren't adequate.

Once he saw she was asleep again, he stepped out in the hall and asked a nurse for another blanket. To her credit, she hustled and produced a heated one for him to spread over Detective Engle.

He got some sleep, the kind where he drifted just below consciousness, but she awakened with a start several more times. At one point, he had the entirely inappropriate thought that they'd both rest better if he climbed onto that bed with her, spooning her body with his, wrapping an arm around her. He could see it: her head resting on his shoulder, his body heat comforting her.

His mouth twitched wryly. Given that she asked him twice more who he was, he could only imagine her reaction to finding a strange man in bed with her.

He presumed if she was married her father or the judge would have said so. But didn't she have a boyfriend who would want to be here?

The next time he stirred and opened his eyes, gray light filtered into the room through the blinds and she was curled up facing him…and watching him.

Her eyes were beautiful, a warm brown that held elusive hints of gold. Not surprisingly given her auburn hair, she had a few freckles that looked like a spice—cinnamon, maybe—sprinkled over her nose.

He cleared any huskiness from his throat. "Do I need to introduce myself again?"

A smile curled her lips. "No, my head feels a little clearer this morning."

"But pounding, I'll bet."

"Yes."

He reminded her to punch the button to up her dose of pain meds and saw how relief softened the grip of her hands on the covers and shoulders that had been too rigid.

They kept looking at each other for a minute. Then the detective said, "You've been here all night."

"I have."

"Surely you get a room when you're going to be anyplace for long."

"Yeah. My boss booked me at the Tulip Motor Inn."

Amusement warmed her eyes. "We do have fancier establishments in town."

"From what he said, mostly bed and breakfasts. I prefer more privacy than that."

"I suppose so." She went quiet for a minute before asking, "Do you know if they plan to let me go home today? Or...well, what kind of injuries I have?"

"Haven't spoken to your doctor, but I do know you had a concussion. You've got some bruising and swelling on your face, not to mention a black eye."

"Lovely." She groped with one hand and pressed a cheekbone, then winced.

"The bomb appears to have been packed with some kind of shrapnel, maybe just nails. That's why your back probably stings."

"I remember that. It was like... I don't know, when a car accelerates too fast and spits gravel at you. It all happened so fast, it's hard to break down in my head. Just...

boom, and a flash that was so bright, I'm surprised it didn't damage my eyesight."

He didn't tell her that was a possibility. A teammate in Iraq had gone home after losing a hand and his vision.

"So...will you tell me what you plan to do?"

"Uh, shave." He scraped a hand over his bristly jaw. "I may even shower."

Her smile rewarded him.

"Got to look my best to greet all those ATF agents who will be showing up any time. I'll be outnumbered, you know. And we federal agents don't always play well together."

"From what I've heard, it's usually the FBI agents who annoy everyone else." Laughter showed in those extraordinary eyes.

"Maybe." More seriously, he said, "It's mostly a matter of personality. Haven't you met local officers and deputies who have an ego problem?"

"Oh, yes. My promotion to detective irked some guys who'd wanted it. I know it's easier for women in law enforcement now than it was a decade ago, but there's still resistance."

"So I've gathered." Nolan felt a strange reluctance to get moving, even though familiar anticipation also ran through him. He needed to be investigating, but he liked this quiet conversation. He liked this woman.

"What time is it?"

When he told her, she said, "I imagine my father will be along soon. He's always an early riser."

"Your mother?"

"She died of breast cancer when I was in high school."

"That's hard on everyone."

"Yes. But long past."

He didn't say anything about the brother who'd also died, but he understood better how frantic her father had felt.

She'd composed her expression when she asked, "Do I need to answer any more questions from you?"

"I'm sure I'll have plenty more later. For example, you may think back to whether you saw anyone in the courthouse right beforehand, familiar or not, or happened to notice a vehicle driving away before you entered, or...?"

She shook her head against the pillow. "Nobody. It was the end of the day. I'd been in the east wing talking to an assistant prosecutor about an upcoming trial. I was almost to my car when I realized I needed a restroom." Now she grimaced. "Both for the obvious reason and because I felt queasy. A flu has been going around."

"How is your stomach this morning?"

She blinked a couple of times, as if it hadn't occurred to her to run a systems check. "Actually, my stomach feels fine. Which is lucky, considering not much else does."

"Good." Reluctant as he was, he pushed himself to his feet. "I'm going head back to the hotel for that shower and shave. I'm looking forward to studying the scene and after that will start with trying to figure out how the package made it onto Judge Anderson's desk."

Roanne—Detective Engle—nodded, but a couple of small furrows formed between her eyebrows. That headache was likely to hang on for a couple of days. "Good luck. I hope I'll be assigned to join you once I'm discharged and back on my feet. I'd like to stay on this." Her mouth crimped. "Unless you consider locals to be more of a nuisance than a help."

They often were, but in this case she seemed sharp... *and* was the closest thing to a witness. "No. Local knowledge is essential, especially in a small city like this." He did mean that. "I'll look forward to working with you."

Her soft voice followed him to the door, where he paused and turned back.

"Thank you. For...last night."

"You're welcome."

Nolan had the uncomfortable feeling that he'd crossed a line last night. It had felt more intimate than he was comfortable with, as if he were the missing boyfriend.

An asinine thought, but...it was hard to keep walking away.

AFTER SHE WAS discharged midday, her dad insisted she spend the night at his place. Roanne had a moment of resistance but hoped she didn't let him see it. He had clung more after Craig's death, and this was a good time to let him have his way. She had been concussed, after all, and despite her curiosity about the scene of the bombing and the feds who probably were swarming it at this moment, she wasn't in any shape to poke her head in. Her knees had a tremor, a woodpecker seemed to be going at her head, and all she really wanted was to sleep.

To sleep, perchance to dream, she thought frivolously, until she remembered that Hamlet had been speculating about death, not afternoon naps.

Her father produced chicken-noodle soup from a box, and to her surprise she swallowed enough to satisfy him. Then she retired to her bedroom, which had remained mostly unchanged since she was a teenager. She'd come home during college a couple of summers to work and stripped down a few posters, packed up books that had been on the shelves and replaced them, but she couldn't remember once sitting down at the desk where she'd done the majority of her homework.

Dad would have been delighted if she'd moved back into her room when she took the job here with the Rosendaal Police Department. After college, she'd worked for a few years for the King County Sheriff's Department, one of the largest police departments in the state, but her father's joy when she came home for a few days eventually had persuaded her that she could make a life here, if only for him.

It still was for him. Friends from her school days were around, but she didn't have much in common with them anymore. She dated occasionally, but men who weren't in law enforcement seemed to be threatened by the idea of a woman who was…and the men *in* law enforcement wanted to assert dominance.

Sort of like Special Agent Cantrell had referred to the relationship with other cops and feds.

Ugh.

Would *he* be different…?

What a ridiculous question. She had no doubt his focus would be absolute.

Still, Roanne liked the little house—more a cottage, really—that she'd bought a couple of years ago. She'd taken up gardening as a remedy against stress and frequently saw tourists braking by her house to admire her tulips and roses and beds full of perennials.

The nap would have been more restful if she hadn't awakened at regular intervals with her ears ringing and her eyes aching. She dragged herself up, grimaced at the sight of herself in the mirror in the bathroom and felt like an old woman when she staggered to the living room.

Her father smiled at her. "Feeling some better?"

"I'm sure I do. Just..."

"Head?"

"Yeah. Did Agent Cantrell call?"

"No. A dozen other people have heard you were hurt and called, including Chief Brenk. He evidently watched from a distance as a crew from the ATF gathered evidence at the courthouse, but they didn't share what they were thinking with him and clearly disapproved of the lack of security for entering, not to mention the lack of cameras."

"I've said the same."

He nodded. "Something tells me there will be some serious upgrades in the near future. The city council won't oppose the expenditure, not after Charles had such a close call."

About time.

"I hope you plan to take a few days off."

There it was: the worry that was so often in his eyes when he watched her or changed the tenor of his voice. He'd probably love it if she made a career about-face and, say, became a teacher instead of carrying a gun and probing for answers so that she could cuff the kind of people he'd rather not acknowledge.

"No, I want to be involved," she said. "If nothing else, I can learn from seeing how federal agents go about an investigation like this. More than that, though, I can't help thinking..." She hesitated.

"This wasn't a one-time thing?"

"Yeah."

He didn't argue, but he didn't like her answer, either. That was a frequent state of affairs between them.

It was a good time for her phone to ring

She pounced on it. "Agent Cantrell?"

"That's me. How are you?"

"Better."

"Uh-huh. Your dad buy that?"

"No, but compared to last night in the hospital, I'm a new woman."

"I thought I'd update you."

"Thank you," she said fervently.

"That was a powerful bomb. It would have destroyed most of the judge's chamber if it had gone off there. In fact, it seems over-built considering it was seemingly intended to kill one man. Marble chipped from walls and floor." He sounded grim. "I think it's close to a miracle that *you* weren't killed."

Letting that pass, Roanne said, "Could that be inexperience? I mean, he didn't know how much flash he needed?"

"It's possible. Maybe he just didn't mind the idea of a couple more people who happened to be in the vicinity dying, too. This was plainly staged to make a statement."

"Yes. Um, I assume you've talked to Judge Anderson. Does he have any thoughts about recent or upcoming trials that this may be linked to?"

"I have, although briefly, and no. We'll talk to people, but a guy who just got out after serving ten years in the Monroe Correctional Institute could have been biding his time. Finding the motive is a nice objective but unrealistic when we know of only one target."

She bit her lip. "You mean, until…"

His voice lowered to a rumble. "Until," he agreed.

Until a second bomb, or even a third one, helped them close in on the perpetrator, or perpetrators.

"I want you to be careful," Cantrell said. "*You* thwarted him. He's not going to like that."

Roanne hoped her father, ostensibly looking for something in the refrigerator, couldn't hear the agent's side of this conversation.

"I'm...aware," she said carefully. "I'll hope to meet the other investigators."

"I thought you may want to. We're sitting down together in conference room C at the courthouse at nine in the morning. If you want me to pick you up—"

"Since my car is still sitting at the curb in front of the courthouse, that may be a good idea. Thank you."

"Do you keep your car in your garage at home?"

She knew where he was going with this and didn't like it. "Yes."

"We'll give it a once-over tomorrow before you so much as unlock."

"How reassuring."

He laughed.

Chapter Three

"Thank you for picking me up." Roanne nestled her laptop on the vehicle floor between her feet, slammed her door shut and reached for the seat belt. Settled, she forced a smile and waved at the still figure standing at the front window of the house.

Imagine if she'd agreed to live at home! How would she ever have gained respect in the department? Kept her sanity?

"Your father want you to stay home today?"

"And every day," she mumbled.

The too-handsome man behind the wheel glanced over his shoulder to check for traffic before easing away from the curb. "I'm not surprised. He got a real scare."

"I know he did." She sighed. "He's never been enthusiastic about my career. He just hides how he feels better sometimes than others."

"Because you're a woman?" Agent Cantrell's voice held the slightest roughness that gave her goosebumps.

"Probably? I think it just came at him out of left field." She frowned. "You must work with female agents."

"Sure. You'll meet one from the ATF today. Agent Krogen can put the pieces of an incendiary device back together like no one I've ever seen. She spreads out every microscopic shred on a table, locks onto it and quits hearing or noticing anyone else in the room. It's fascinating to watch her work. She has this laser focus. All those pieces make up a jigsaw puzzle to her, and she sees where everything fits."

"You respect her."

He sounded surprised. "Yes. You'll like her. In fact, I asked her to arrange for one of their people to take a look at your car to make sure it wasn't rigged."

"I...remember you saying you'd do that, but the bomber probably isn't interested in me at all. Why would he be?"

"It was unlikely." He braked downtown and frowned at the red light. "Not so much now."

His assessment gave her a tiny chill, as if she'd swallowed an ice cube that proceeded to slither its way down her throat and through her system.

"You...made your point. I've arrested enough people who don't like me. What's one more?"

If he heard the bravado beneath what was meant to be confidence, Agent Cantrell didn't say anything.

He parked in the lot behind the courthouse, got out and gazed critically around while he waited for her. "This lot should have additional security. Right now, anybody can drive in, do a car prowl, wait for people leaving court."

Roanne glared at him over the hood of his SUV. "It's well lit. And yes, I've been pushing for increased security surrounding the courthouse since I started work here. In some ways, this is still a sleepy town, but crime spikes every year during the tulip festival, and we have a lot of newcomers living here now, people drawn by lower real estate prices and willing to commute to Boeing in Everett or even to Seattle. In theory, we're in the rain shadow of the Olympic Mountains, too. Compare our annual rainfall to towns a little farther east and you'll become a believer."

"It's a nice town," he conceded.

Roanne heard the dubious note in the compliment and assumed Rosendaal was a little too quaint for his tastes. She couldn't argue that the city had grabbed on to tourism with enthusiasm or even desperation; half the businesses in town used *tulip* or *daffodil* or even *crocus* in the name. Tulips in every color were painted on the windows, carved into wood signs or even plastered on a couple of enormous banners that hung at every intersection of the main street.

She'd have toned it down herself, but she liked the good cheer, so she didn't want to hear any criticism from him. After locking his vehicle remotely, he joined her. She looked straight ahead, even though his gaze landed on her.

"Definitely a black eye," he observed.

"Really? I didn't notice."

He chuckled. "You couldn't have plastered on enough makeup to cover those bruises."

She wouldn't tell him she'd tried, looked at herself in the mirror, then washed it all off. Why should she hide the damage? A degree of tartness tinged her internal question. Some of those jerks who didn't like her promotion could see her and weep.

She quit thinking about how she looked and concentrated instead on disguising her many aches as she climbed the dozen steps to the back doors of the courthouse. Agent Cantrell opened the door and held it for her. Two uniformed guards stepped closer but recognized him immediately and, of course, her, too.

"Detective." One of them nodded. "Agent Cantrell."

"I can't believe the county has been this lax," Cantrell grumbled as they continued down a long hall.

"As you've already said."

She felt this glance, too, although she didn't understand why. Maybe it was the sharpness of his gaze. Roanne suspected he was good at reading intentions and buried emotions, if not actual thoughts.

He paused at the elevator and pushed the button, presumably to save her from having to mount another flight of stairs. And to think how careful she'd been to hold herself straight, walk evenly despite a hip and butt that hurt, and suppress every whimper. But he'd seen her yesterday. He had to know she hadn't bounded out of bed this morning, feeling as fresh as a daisy.

No, as a spring tulip, she thought, a little grumpily.

As they stepped from the elevator, she heard voices down the hall spilling from the conference room. Half a dozen people sat around the long table that filled most of the space. Almost all had open laptops in front of them, although a few lingered by the side table where coffee was available along with doughnuts.

"Would you like a cup of coffee?" her escort asked quietly.

"Yes, but I can get—"

"I'm offering. Go sit down."

Roanne made herself say "Thank you," wondering when she'd become so ungracious.

She chose an empty chair near one end of the table and smiled politely at the guy to her right. His grizzled hair was cut military short, and he wore cargo pants and a black polo shirt with the ATF symbol on the chest.

Everybody was looking at her. Exhibit A. She introduced herself and tried to take in all the names as they did the same, although she felt sure some were going in one ear and out the other, as her mother used to say.

She looked around. "Chief Brenk isn't here?"

Agent Long—she thought she had that right—said, "He promised to try to make it. I suspect his messages are piling up faster than he can return calls. He figured you could represent the city."

She'd guessed as much. A town this size had a total of four detectives, and it made sense to leave the investigation in her hands considering she'd been an active participant from the start. So to speak.

The one other woman at the table was, obviously, Agent Krogen. Maybe in her forties, with blond hair pulled back into a ponytail, she eyed Roanne. "I'm sending photos to everyone. If you'll give me your email address…"

Roanne did and heard a few pings a moment later.

Once everyone was sitting, Roanne chose to be assertive in the absence of her police chief. This *was* her town. "Thank you all for coming and getting here so fast. I've never been involved in a bomb or even arson investigation, but I gather this is what you all do."

"Yep," said the man at her side. "We live for it. Especially Sharon."

A ripple of laughter circled the table.

An older guy from the ATF sat at one end of the table, while Cantrell sat at the other, right beside her. Was that chance or protocol?

The ATF agent studied her. "I'm the head of this unit from the EEO program. Stands for *Explosives Enforcement Officers*," he expanded.

She nodded. She'd have liked to have done more research before this meeting, but yesterday her eyes started to cross every time she made an effort to concentrate on her laptop. Whatever Agent Cantrell said, she had a suspicion she'd find herself set aside as the investigation expanded. Truthfully, she didn't have any particular skill set to bring to the table.

The lead guy glanced around. "If there are no objections, I think we should start with Detective Engle's experience."

She saw encouragement on Cantrell's face and said, "I'll do my best. I'd be a lot more helpful if I could slow down time, but…"

Again, she heard amusement.

They listened, broke in with questions, tried to get her to freeze-frame this instant or another. They wanted her to walk them through those few seconds at the scene.

The female ATF agent scrutinized her as if trying to see inside her. "Honestly," she said, "I don't know how you escaped with such relatively minor injuries."

Roanne winced. Apparently keeping her heavily wrapped wrist below table height hadn't fooled anyone.

They hurried to expand on their point of view. The bomb had been powerful enough, the shock waves should have punctured her ear drums, sinuses, even intestines. She didn't want to think about that.

She admitted that the ER doc had expected to find her ear drums ruptured and had checked them several times as if he couldn't believe they weren't. Something was said about hollow parts of the bodies not resisting the force of the explosion as well as solid tissue.

"I know that after I threw the package as far as I could," she said awkwardly, "I at least had in mind jumping back toward the office. I know I wrapped my arms around my head as I did that, so they must have protected my ears. I, um, do have penetrating wounds on my back—"

"Nobody told me," Agent Krogen interrupted with what sounded like annoyance. "That was going to be my next question. I suppose I can't ask you to pull your shirt up and show us."

They all stared at her. She stared back. What the heck.

Carefully, in deference to her many aches, she stood, pulled her shirt from her waistband and turned her back on the table. Nolan Cantrell was suddenly beside her, lifting her shirt when her shoulders protested any such activity.

Murmurs of interest were followed by a couple of gentle touches. Then he pulled her shirt back down, smiled crookedly and pushed her chair in behind her when she lowered herself stiffly.

"It appears as if you had your back entirely turned when the bomb ignited," someone said.

"I...don't know," she admitted.

One of the other men frowned at her. "You took several running steps out of the office into the open, heaved the package as far as you could and somehow turned around and jumped *back*?"

Getting annoyed, Roanne said, "Like I said, it happened in what felt like a matter of seconds. I didn't really *think*. I just reacted."

"Well, you look athletic," a thinner, less intense man observed.

She half expected somebody to suggest she strip to her bra and panties so they could inspect her muscle tone. She must have bristled, because Agent Cantrell laid a hand on her thigh beneath the table.

"I was an athlete," she said shortly. "Soccer and track and field. I was a high jumper in high school and at the University of Washington, where I reached the NCAA finals. So if there's one thing I do well, it's jump."

"You must have learned to fall, too," someone said thoughtfully.

"And if I remember right," Sharon Krogen observed, "high jumpers twist mid-jump. Go up facing the bar, somehow twist so they can arch and lift the hips over it, then fall onto their backs."

"That's right."

"It sounds to me," Cantrell said, "that Detective Engle was almost uniquely qualified to survive an event that would have left even the usual law enforcement officer with extensive injuries."

"You must not have been wearing a vest." That was the thin guy.

"No. This was one of the rare circumstances where I think I was lucky I *hadn't* put it on. It might have protected me in one way, but I suspect it would have limited my movements."

"Yes, indeed." Agent Krogen sounded energized. "I wish we had it on film."

Roanne's friendly FBI agent snorted. She kept her mouth shut.

They were seemingly satisfied enough to move on. Krogen, whose stated specialty was collecting every piece of an exploded device and somehow almost reassembling it, had set up a lab in Everett, a half hour south of Rosendaal because of her need for equipment not available locally. The photos she'd sent to their laptops were sharp, displaying the scene, the camera first looking at the landing from near the top of the steps, then from down one of the halls. Other photos broke down into details. She had been scrupulous to separate anything that wasn't part of the bomb had been gathered and had made astonishing progress on putting it together to the point where they could have a spirited discussion about the bomb maker's experience and whether his device closely resembled others they'd seen.

Krogen said, "My gut says he isn't as sophisticated as this appears. Yeah, it went off, not always the case for a beginner, but we all know how many recipes are readily available online for building this kind of device. My feeling is this one is identical to others I've seen before."

Cantrell leaned forward. "Doesn't mean we don't need to scour records for a previous, if less successful, bomb. Could be a couple of counties away. Say it didn't go off or was dismantled."

"There are several bomb squads in western Washington," someone agreed.

Talk continued over Roanne's head. She found the quick arguments and exchanges of information fascinating despite not understanding everything that was said.

Target selection was deemed critical. That she did get, no trouble. Figure out who wanted to hurt the victim, you could narrow down who had actually tried. That was true for almost every investigation—but given the judge's profession, the list of potentially aggrieved individuals was vast.

How had the package been delivered? She gathered that was at the top of Cantrell's list. They skated over the mention of normal clues for a crime like this; there were no footprints, tire prints or camera systems. If a fingerprint had been left on a fragment of the bomb, Krogen had yet to find it.

"I think we need to look at court employees," Cantrell added in a hard voice. "Almost everyone who works in the courthouse—"

"Or has ready access," Roanne pointed out.

He tipped his head. "Or has ready access, as the guards seem to approve entry without question, could have brought this package in a briefcase or tote bag, then waited until it was quiet upstairs to insert it in the pile of mail waiting for Judge Anderson."

"We're sure it didn't come through the US mail?"

"We don't believe so." Cantrell raised his brows at Krogen. "Have you found any shred that suggests postage was on the package?"

"Not so far."

"Doesn't the judge have a secretary who opens his mail?" Agent Donahue asked.

"I...don't know," Roanne had to admit.

"You're just about the only person we know who couldn't have delivered the device," Donahue grumbled.

How nice to know she'd been under suspicion. "I could have stopped by earlier."

"The guards said no."

Wonderful. They really had looked at her for this. As they should have, she admitted grudgingly but didn't appreciate it nonetheless. But who knew? Maybe her plans included dying in the spectacular explosions that also killed the superior court judge.

As she simmered, a warm hand engulfed her tightly balled fist. Cantrell didn't turn his head, but he was reading her just fine, and she understood the message he was sending. She was sorry when he withdrew his hand.

She'd save for later wondering why he *was* being so friendly.

Fast-paced conversation turned to the hunt for DNA, fingerprints, hair or fibers found with the bomb materials. Krogen was making up a list of materials that could be traced to a store like the local Home Depot.

Once she had produced a "shopping list" of components, Agent Donahue would head the attempt to determine where those components had been purchased—and whether that purchase had included enough to manufacture more devices.

They agreed to leave the judge to Cantrell. "This almost has to be linked to one of his trials, prior or forthcoming," the thin, quieter man observed.

Cantrell nodded. "We've started the discussion, but we need to drill in on his calendar, past and future. I'll include Detective Engle in this aspect of the investigation. She knows him well and has appeared in court any number of times before him. I want to know when he last opened his mail and whether he typically does it himself. We'll need to talk to everyone who had reason to come and go into the courthouse the past few days as well. We need as complete a list as soon as possible. Hopefully some puzzling names pop."

Roanne had been wondering when someone would politely thank her for her intercession and let her know that she now lacked any useful expertise.

Which was true, in a way, but she wondered how often a breakthrough in an investigation like this came down to asking questions and listening for something the person didn't even know they knew.

If that made sense.

"We need to ask the judge who he remembers seeing coming and going from his office, too," she said. "If somebody had surprised him, he'd have thought to have mention them, but what if a note was left on his desk? You read it, crumple it up and throw it away without giving it another thought."

Nolan nodded at her. "I'll leave that to you."

"Okay," the guy at the head of the table said. "Let's meet again tomorrow—same time, same place. But you know the drill. If you learn *anything* of significance, share."

"Yeah, yeah."

He scowled toward one of the men who hadn't said much. "You know the chances are good that this wasn't a one-off."

Roanne felt another chill. His belief there'd be another attempt to kill Judge Anderson didn't surprise her. The big question was whether there might be other targets.

Either way, the reminder was unsettling.

Chapter Four

Not surprisingly, Nolan and Roanne were informed that courtroom trials, depositions and hearings had been postponed to prevent gawkers from getting in the way and to allow security to be ramped up. Having the calendar backed up was going to make for a mess down the line, but unless and until federal agents could guarantee that no other bomb lurked, untouched as yet, somewhere in the building, they hadn't had much choice. Roanne understood that a handler and bomb-sniffing dog borrowed from Seattle PD were to go over the courthouse tomorrow.

They were also informed that Judge Anderson was working from home today. Much as he wanted to talk to the judge, Nolan insisted that first his priority was a discussion regarding future security. Roanne knew he planned to speak at the next county council meeting. In the meantime, he reamed the court administrator and the head of security. He made plain what had to be done—and what precautions would be taken in the immediate future to protect court support personnel, judges, witnesses, janitors and individuals on trial. Roanne was careful to remain expressionless. Nobody liked people who went around saying *I told you so*.

As they left a deeply distressed roomful of people,

however, Nolan cocked an eyebrow at her but hesitated when she turned toward the back of the building.

"Do we drive together? If not, I'll head out to my car."

He scowled. "Of course you're coming with me. Unless you think the judge will hold back because of his relationship with you?"

She would never admit how overpowering his physical presence was. Confined in the front seat of his vehicle, she was even more conscious of everything about him—the bulk of his shoulders, the muscles in his forearms, the tuft of dark hair revealed by the open collar of his shirt. She'd tried hard not to let her gaze drop to his powerful thighs…or anything else in that vicinity.

Answer him. Calm and cool.

"No. He's far more accepting of my job than my father is. I appear before him routinely."

"Then let's go see him."

Falling in step with him, she asked, "Shall I call?"

"I texted earlier. He responded with his address."

Nolan hopped up behind the wheel with a lithe ease she envied, fired up the engine and looked at her. "Left? Right?"

She put on her seat belt and gave directions. They hadn't escaped town when he swore under his breath.

"The town isn't big enough to have backups like this!"

Surprised, she said, "Oh, this is nothing. Wait a few more weeks, once all the tulips are fully in bloom. Tulip festival—remember?"

He growled something else but also seemed to be paying attention to vast acres of yellow daffodils in bloom, most preceding the tulips. Smaller fields of crocuses in shades of purple and lavender provided accent. Cars slowed to a crawl so everyone could crane their necks.

Some drivers pulled to the side so everyone could get out and take pictures. The two-lane rural highway was not wide enough to safely allow parking on the shoulders, but local deputies wouldn't be ticketing any of them, either. The flowers in bloom were the lifeblood of this area.

Seeming to resign himself, Cantrell glanced at her. "What did you think?"

"About? Oh, you mean the meeting." She took the question seriously. "I was impressed," she said after thinking. "There were some bright people in that room. Honestly, I didn't understand everything that was said. I suppose you do—"

"I do only because of my army service. When I chose not to re-up, I'd have looked closely at the offer the ATF made me if it hadn't gotten to the point that I hate things that blow up."

She worried her lower lip. "I can see how that would happen. I'm going to have nightmares just from the one experience, and nobody died."

By the grace of God. The room full of people this morning seemed certain that without her background as a track-and-field athlete, they would have been picking up pieces of *her* yesterday.

Something like a shudder passed through her. She hoped he didn't notice.

"If nothing else," she said, "I'll think of this investigation as a gift. I probably won't have a chance again to work with specialists from *two* federal agencies."

Nolan grinned. "You do know that most local cops hate it when we step in."

"It hasn't been like that so far."

"And won't be, if I can help it. Let me know if anyone turns smug and condescending."

"I can take care of that kind of problem myself," Roanne told him.

"Well, it may get worse. If a second bomb explodes in the near future, I won't be the only FBI agent in town. Worse yet, it's possible agents from the whole alphabet soup of federal agencies will appear."

"That's when egos start playing bumper car?" she asked with amusement.

"We're a little more polite than that." His expression mostly showed amusement, however.

A few minutes later, he asked, "Flood land?" Apparently, the obvious had finally occurred to him.

It was true. The Skagit River valley was flat as a pancake. Roanne pointed out how many of the older homes with acreage were built high to allow for seasonal flooding without water getting into the houses. The rich soil, she told him was why agriculture thrived in the county.

The judge owned a sprawling two-story home perched on one of the ridges that allowed a view of Puget Sound.

"Nice place," Cantrell observed.

Roanne nodded. "Dad says Uncle Charles and his wife are thinking of selling. This house is bigger than they need, now that both boys are gone. I think they've hesitated because Lars is, uh—"

"The judge told me about his diagnosis. Said he's married now and has a good job."

"Still." What parent could not worry about the future when a child had been difficult to raise and unlikely to fully fit in with other people?

Gravel crunched.

"Do you want me to stay in the background?" she asked.

He parked, set the brake and turned off the engine.

"No, we have no reason to look at him as a suspect. If he's comfortable with you, he's likely to be more forthcoming."

So she wasn't to be muzzled—not yet, she thought, reaching for the door handle.

NOLAN PAID ATTENTION to Roanne's hesitation after she opened the passenger door. The ground was an easy reach for him with his long legs, but she probably felt as if she was having to dismount from the horse in Olympic gymnastics, and that wasn't her sport. She succeeded in landing solidly and pretending it hadn't been an effort at all.

He liked her pride.

Judge Anderson had the door open to greet them by the time they reached the porch. Aware as he was of her injuries, he gently hugged Roanne, who hugged him back with seeming cordiality.

"Mary wanted to hang around to see you, but I shooed her out the door to get groceries. I don't want her hearing more than is necessary."

"I'd suggest you don't share much of what we talk about with her, either," Nolan suggested.

The judge gave him a sharp glance but didn't comment. He led them to a dining nook off a spacious kitchen, where his laptop sat open and additional files and what seemed to be a few pages of his court calendar lay on the table covering. He poured two cups of coffee for them, replenished his own, then sat down.

"As you can see, I've started looking for anything recent that could have resulted in this level of rage."

"Unfortunately, something like that doesn't necessarily leap out at you," Nolan said. "It's the saying about the eye of the beholder. What's a slightly embarrassing misdemeanor to one man may be humiliation and the threat of a job loss to another. Or a more personal loss."

Judge Anderson's gaze challenged him. "Granted, but we still need to try to narrow down possibilities, wouldn't you agree?"

"I do. Just cautioning you."

They started with the judge explaining that typically he did open his own mail. Much of it lacked urgency, so he then passed it on to an assistant who made appointments and answered questions on his behalf.

That out of the way, they spent what Nolan wanted to believe was a productive several hours working through appearances before Judge Anderson in the past couple of months. A few were minor, but not most. As a superior court judge—the only one in this county—he primarily oversaw the more serious crimes. Murder, rape, assault, embezzlement. Roanne didn't appear surprised, but of course, she'd probably made some of these arrests.

"The problem is," the judge commented, "in most of the worst of these instances, the perpetrator is in prison. Even if they weren't, I've got to say most are more likely to lie in wait with a baseball bat or a handgun than fiddle with electronic and chemical components. I'm well educated, but I'm not sure that, even with instructions, I could build something like that."

Nolan could have but saw Roanne nodding.

"I never liked science classes." She and the older man exchanged rueful smiles. "Somehow, the word *rage* doesn't quite go with this kind of remote attack, either. It suggests..." She hesitated.

"An organized perpetrator."

"Right. I mean, wouldn't an angry man want to lash out in person? At least *see* what happens?"

"Fairly often, it turns out they *are* nearby, waiting for the emergency vehicles to drive up flashing lights and blaring sirens." Nolan sighed. "Arson isn't my area, but a not-so-secret truth about incendiary devices is that many are built by firefighters. Their excitement is responding to the blaze, whether building or wild land. Depending, a big fire that leads to a full callout may bump their paychecks, too."

"Ugh. I've read that." Roanne frowned. "I noticed in the meeting earlier that everyone used the pronoun *he*."

"That's because women almost never are responsible. It's not a crime that appeals to them, for whatever reason."

"Blowing things up does seem like a male preoccupation," she said dryly.

Nolan kept his mouth shut. He'd blown up plenty of devices that couldn't be dismantled easily. Had he gotten a charge out of it in the early days? If so, he didn't remember. Yeah, there'd been fireworks when he was a kid, too, but he mostly suppressed those memories. Picturing an explosion caused a knot of dread to tighten beneath his breastbone.

"Anything jump out at you?" the judge asked, looking between them.

"Well…" Roanne reached out to touch a line on one calendar. "That one was ugly."

Nolan tipped his head to see. *Ugly* was the right word. The guy had brutally murdered his in-laws and, evidence suggested, gone to the home his wife had kicked him out of with the intent of killing her, too.

"He's locked up in Walla Walla for thirty years," the judge pointed out.

"Yes, but there was a suggestion that he hadn't acted alone," she reminded Anderson. "We couldn't prove it, but his wife was scared enough that she disappeared. She told me she knew—what was his name?" Crinkles furrowed her usually smooth forehead and rearranged a few freckles. "It was the husband's brother, glowering at the back of the courtroom. Andrew," she said suddenly. "Andrew Billman. It wouldn't hurt to track him down and see what he's been up to."

"I saw him up in Mount Vernon six months or so ago." The judge frowned. "Kind of gave me a turn. I'm not sure he saw me, though."

Nolan made a note. "We'll track him down."

They threw around ideas, but most cases had been straightforward murders: domestic, bar brawls, mental breaks that ended more tragically than they needed to. His gut said none of those had led to this carefully planned attempt on the judge's life.

He sat back. "Since we have only one projected victim at this point, we need to talk about even remote possibilities that are personal, that don't have anything to do with your job."

The judge's mouth fell open. "Good God, I can't imagine. I've been married happily to the same woman for thirty years, we raised two children together and neither of us ever cheated. Mary doesn't make enemies," he said. "Everyone loves her."

Nolan didn't say *Uh-huh* out loud, because he had a more twisted view of the world. Maybe Mary was a maternal, warm-hearted woman who had never insulted a soul, but in his experience, people didn't always see beyond their own certainties.

Judge Anderson excused himself to take a call and stepped out on the back deck to talk.

Nolan raised his brows at Roanne. "I didn't want to

say this in front of him, but what about his sons? Does the youngest resent his older brother's success? Maybe simmered for years while everyone was cheering on—what's his name?"

"Erik. I really don't believe it was like that. Lars is a sweetie. I...actually went to his senior prom with him. He didn't have a girlfriend then, and, you know, we'd grown up together. Sometimes he's kind of goofy, but he's as smart as Erik. When I see him, he tells me about podcasts he listens to on the road, and he's a big reader. You've never seen anyone in your life more excited than he was when his little boy was born."

Nolan filed away her description. Smart *and* resentful would make this his kind of crime.

"Any other family?"

"Not in the area. The judge's sister and her family live in Northern California. She's a state representative." Roanne smiled. "Uncle Charles can't imagine why anyone would want to step into constant strife."

"Like his job is sunshine and roses."

"That's true." She wrinkled her nose. "Mine isn't, either, and I'm sure yours is even less so, and we got ourselves into those jobs."

He grimaced. "I can't argue." It sounded as if the judge was winding up his conversation and would be back in with them any minute. "What's the most unusual trial he's presided over?"

Her face went oddly still, waving a red flag for him. "We had a tabloid-worthy trial...oh, two years ago? You may have read about it at the time. We had—and still have—our own cult living on land not too far out of town."

"A cult." Damn. He did recall that. He'd been deep in

something else at the time, but law enforcement taking on a cult wasn't an everyday occurrence, either.

"They'd been around for something like ten years. Not when I was growing up, so I didn't know any of the kids. They wanted to homeschool, but the district put its foot—feet?—down and insisted the children be educated among all the other kids. I guess a lot of them seemed pretty normal, even embarrassed because of their living situation. Turned out they weren't permitted to take part in extracurricular activities, including sports, but, you know, that usually requires parents being willing to carpool, and so that didn't grab anybody's attention, either."

Nolan waited.

"The cult leader was weirdly charismatic—I have to admit that. Burning eyes, a voice that effortlessly carried. When he was talking, it was hard to look away."

"He?"

"Oh. He'd taken the name Theodoros, Fedor for short. Theodoros in Greek mythology is the gift of God."

"And did he have them all convinced he could offer them salvation in the afterlife?"

"Something like that. It was communal living, and people handed over their entire life's savings to him."

"I see. How did these folks make a living?"

"Well, that's how everyone got complacent. A bunch of cult members held jobs in town, just like other locals. A couple of women volunteered regularly at the food bank, as saintly as you could want. They were discouraged from trying to pray with the customers—"

"Recruit them, you mean?" he said drily.

"Probably."

Judge Anderson stepped back in, closing the French door behind him. "Did I miss anything?"

"Detective Engle is telling me about your home-grown cult."

"Ah. That was more colorful than most actions that came before me. Still." He shrugged. "Fedor is behind bars and will be for years."

"But the cult is hanging on?"

Roanne answered. "Dwindling. Fedor—whose real name, by the way, was Dwayne Knepper—was forced to give money back to his faithful, although somehow much of the money was gone. Still, probably half the families have moved away, last I heard. I haven't been out there in ages, but I gather some didn't have much money in the first place and can't see what to do going forward."

"Any other leadership?"

"Several people high up in the structure answered questions in court. Con men, one and all," the judge said with distaste.

"They had a lot to lose," Nolan pointed out.

"Sure. But we're not mid-trial. What's done is done. Were any of them really devoted enough to their fallen leader to come after me motivated by nothing but a taste for revenge? This much later? I don't see it."

Nolan glanced at Roanne, who made a face. "I'm... less certain that's true—fanatics scare me—but it does seem unlikely."

"Does he have family?"

"I couldn't locate anyone at the time," she said.

"Just out of curiosity," Nolan asked, "what brought Fedor down?"

"From what I've read, the usual. He took all the money, and he required the women to service him on demand. The husbands/partners just had to suck it up if they didn't like it."

That was a common thread undermining cults.

"Plus," she continued, "he and his stalwart faithful were beating people, molesting kids, all kinds of awful things. A ten-year-old girl died after a beating. They managed to hide what happened for a while, but word eventually got out. That was the breaking point."

"And the rest of them just let that happen." He could still be staggered by human behavior.

"I guess a few protested. People probably left the cult, but none of the adults spilled the beans. Enforcers wandering around with guns probably had a deterrent effect. It was kids who couldn't keep their mouths shut."

"I think we need to look into this cult," Nolan said slowly. "I don't quite see how it could relate to the bombing, but we'll throw it out to the team."

"Doesn't it take *some* training to be able to build a device like that?" Judge Anderson asked.

"It's common for a perpetrator to have a background in one of the sciences. An engineer, a chemist, at least a mechanic. But who's to say someone who'd gotten sucked in hadn't at least taught science in school—or had an especially enthusiastic science teacher big on DIY."

The judge promised to copy the trial transcript and leave it at the courthouse by five o'clock the next day so Nolan could read it.

Intrigued by the possibilities, Nolan, too, was doubtful. Bomb makers were usually loners. Sometimes revenge was part of the motive, but there were other instances where victims were almost random. The bastards just got off by maiming and killing.

He cautioned Judge Anderson to make his personal safety a priority. He might even consider visiting his son in Seattle, say, until the courthouse reopened. Nolan was blunt that he felt a second attempt was possible, maybe even likely.

They thanked the judge. Nolan went to her side of the SUV to offer to boost her up, but she gave him a narrow-eyed, don't-you-dare look that had him hiding a grin as he circled to his own side. She was a cop. Of course she didn't expect other law enforcement agents, local or federal, to treat her with chivalry.

Once they started back to town, he said, "I don't know about you, but I'm starved."

"I wonder what the others did. They may have had sandwiches delivered."

"Let's not join the crowd. I don't want to get swept up in half a dozen theories yet."

"Only mine?"

"You know the people in this town. You're less likely to have a brilliant idea that isn't even remotely supported by facts."

Roanne made a face again. "If I had one, would you listen?"

Nolan turned his head sharply. "I'd listen."

"Well, I wish I had anything *approaching* a brilliant idea." She made plain that she was done with the conversation by throwing out suggestions for cafés and pizza parlors.

They agreed on one and finished the agonizingly slow drive back to town in silence. He couldn't quite figure out why this silence felt…uneasy.

Chapter Five

Eating a gyro at a café and trying hard not to allow an unsightly drip onto her uniform shirt, Roanne answered whenever Nolan asked a question but otherwise held her tongue.

She was having a crisis of faith—in herself. She did know many Rosendaal citizens. That was the sum total of her contribution to this investigation, given that she hadn't understood fifty percent of the discussion about the bomb's innards this morning and that she felt outclassed by the quiet, stern man sitting across the table from her. She couldn't begin to guess what he'd consider most important to do next.

After they finished their lunches, he paid, shaking his head when she pulled out her wallet, then asked, "How are you? Don't say 'Fine.' Be honest."

"Oh." Strangely, her aches and pains had been the last thing on her mind since they talked to the judge. "I... Not bad. Headache. In fact, I'll take some ibuprofen before we move on."

His gaze appeared relaxed, but she thought that was deceptive. Inclining his head, he said, "What do you see as the priority?"

She was a capable investigator. She was. Although what

came out of her mouth surprised her. "Locate Andrew Billman. Talk to him."

"This is the brother."

She nodded.

"I won't argue."

"Get lists of every person anyone saw enter the courthouse in the past couple of days."

"You don't think we should go further back than that?"

"The bomb could have been brought into the building any time, but then it would have to have been stashed."

"In a locker? A desk drawer?"

"That would work, but how long would you dare leaving it sitting around without someone noticing it? Asking about it, or giving it a shake? That scenario suggests two people are involved. Plus, you'd have to have a lot of confidence it wouldn't go off on its own unexpectedly."

"I'll concede that."

This was the obvious, but she felt she had to say it anyway. "It had to have been inserted into Judge Anderson's pile of mail the day it went off. He'd have noticed it if it had been there the previous day or even that morning. I mean, it stuck out like a sore thumb. And the fact that several pieces of normal, uninteresting mail were placed on top of it tells me that whoever this is had to be in the judge's chamber not long before he finished with hearings for the day."

"I agree," Agent Cantrell said. "That window is helpful. I suggest we go back to the courthouse and interview every person who worked Monday and Tuesday this week. We can start a search for Billman while we're there."

Out in his vehicle, she was fastening her seat belt when he said, "Is something wrong?"

Roanne stiffened. Did a cloud of doubt hang over

her? "No." *Oh, be honest.* "I'm just feeling a little overwhelmed. Whoever made that bomb could be anyone! Uncle Charles has had a long career. He was a prosecutor, you know. What if somebody has been nursing a serious case of hate for fifteen years? We can't possibly investigate everyone who may blame him for whatever went wrong."

One corner of Cantrell's mouth twitched, but his gaze remained steady. "No, we can't. We whittle down possibilities—and hope Sharon comes up with a fingerprint or a drop of blood."

"I thought she'd already thoroughly looked through what she gathered."

"In the sense that she knows how the bomb was meant to work—how it *did* work—yes, she has. But scrutinizing every tiny bit of pipe or the shrapnel or even the wisps remaining from the book of matches—"

"That's how it was set?"

He smiled crookedly. "Weren't you there this morning?"

Roanne gave up on her pride. "I think I tuned out since I don't have any idea how a bomb like that is made. Especially when it was stuffed into such a small box. That was a lot of force."

Some emotion shadowed his face momentarily. "You'd know." He reached for the ignition and said, "All we can do is start and keep on going."

"You think there'll be a repeat."

Agent Cantrell glanced sidelong at her. "I hope I'm wrong, but I do. If you hate one man, would you set out to learn how to build a sophisticated explosive device just to knock him off? There are so many other ways to kill a man from a distance. On the other hand, if you're planning to take care of several people you think need to die, this may hold more appeal. It's showy, which could be gratifying. God knows this one went off in a spectacular fashion. The judge didn't get hurt, but that's not because of any failing on the part of the bomb maker."

He paused, and she filled in what he was thinking. *The failing was because of* her.

"He could have already put together other devices, but I'm guessing he wanted to test one first. He may think he can improve on the design. Make some that are more powerful. Ones that don't stand out to the naked eye. He could even be considering other triggers. Car bombs aren't uncommon. A few years ago, a serial bomber in Atlanta, Georgia, set up one with a trip wire across a sidewalk. Practically invisible." He shook his head. "I hope the judge took my cautions seriously." He turned in to the courthouse parking lot, chose a slot, braked and killed the engine. Because he didn't reach for his seat belt, she sat still, too, waiting.

She couldn't have looked away from his intense blue eyes if she'd *heard* a boom. Roanne was ashamed to be so conscious of how attractive he was. She had to focus on the job.

"I need you to take my concerns seriously, too." Agent Cantrell's low, slightly gritty voice held a grim tone she didn't think she'd heard from him before. "Do you understand me? Don't go for walks. Don't open a door or window without studying it carefully. Not a move you make can be unthinking, casual." He made an odd sound in his throat. "This is why I'd rather hunt just about any other kind of criminal. I hate bombs."

Roanne startled herself by reaching out to lay her hand on his forearm, tense beneath the white dress shirt. "I'll be careful. I promise. You know if something happens, it's *not* your fault. Right?"

He stirred in his seat, rolling his shoulders as if to relieve tension. Tone clipped now, he said, "Not sure I agree with that. But let's get to work."

INSIDE, THEY FOUND that all security guards had been summoned to be available for interviews. Aggravated by this need to protect Roanne that had reared up in Nolan almost from the moment he saw her in that hospital bed, he didn't feel as cool-headed as usual. A pat from her hand and breezy assurance that he wasn't responsible for her hadn't even dented the angry, stubborn streak he usually hid so well.

When he suggested they interview the guards together rather than separately, Roanne bristled but, to her credit, kept her mouth shut, only dipping her head in unhappy agreement.

A waiting room had been turned over to them. Instead of calling in the first guard, Nolan stepped far enough into the room to believe they wouldn't be overheard. Raising his brows, he said, "What is it?"

"We could move a lot faster if we divided them up."

"You're right. But with two of us, we have a better chance of catching a tiny sign that someone is hiding something. Plus, and you're not going to like this, I'm aware you know most if not all these men and women. I gather you like them. Are you capable of stepping back and thinking even folks who are nice on the surface can hold secrets? Resentment? Remember that everyone we're going to talk to today knows the judge."

"You're suggesting he could have cut someone off from

a job opportunity. Come down hard on a wife or husband or kid."

"He could have sexually molested someone."

Her mouth opened and closed a couple of times. Nolan could even sympathize. She didn't just *like* Judge Charles Anderson, she loved him. But she was also honest enough with herself to know that he was right. They had to seriously investigate the possibility that he'd made enemies he might not have wanted to admit to.

"We should find out whether anybody has been fired and if so, whether the judge had anything to do with it." Looking unhappy, Roanne wrinkled her nose. "I may be too close to people we talk to."

"But the fact that you know them better than I do also gives you an advantage. A tiny misstep may nag at you, when I don't notice it."

She made a face at him and puffed out a breath that stirred tiny hairs that had been escaping whatever was confining her richly colored hair to the back of her head. "Fine. You're absolutely right. In fact—"

When she stopped, he cocked an eyebrow.

"Just before the bomb went off, I'd planned to talk to a county councilman who has been accused of sexual harassment, at the least. It's not as if I don't know even picturesque towns with quaint windmills and tulips presenting a sunny image to the world have dark undersides." She tapped her temple. "Which reminds me, I'd better get someone else to talk to him."

Nolan smiled at her, even as he wished he wasn't so conscious of her tall, graceful body, that thick, wavy hair he wanted to touch, her expressive eyes and a stubbornness that matched his own.

Maybe once this investigation was closed, he'd call her. In the meantime, he needed to keep his hands to himself.

"Let's get started," he said gruffly and went to the door.

This was the tedious part. One after another, worried employees took a seat across the table from Nolan and Roanne. Some looked scared, while some were perturbed by what they saw as their own failings. A few gave him momentary pause, but nothing jumped out. One recently hired guard became sullen at the question, guaranteeing Nolan made a mental note of his name.

Roanne tapped the keyboard of her laptop to fill in a spreadsheet listing every single person who had come and gone and when they had been in the courthouse. Unfortunately, who would be able to remember every person they'd seen in the past two days, including some people they knew well enough to have done no more than nod in passing?

As apparently had happened when Roanne entered the courthouse.

Even assuming this list was complete, they were left with plenty of research to be done. Guards had screened and even patted down witnesses, jurors, and friends and family of the individuals being tried. They didn't always know, or remember, the names. At most, the associated trials, and often not even those.

Nolan made a note to requests names and contact numbers of all those jurors and witnesses.

Who might the guards have seen who wasn't associated with a current legal action? Some of them seemed to struggle over that. Defense attorneys, prosecutors, employees like bailiffs and clerks, court administrators, judges and probation counselors involved with the juvenile court—those were the people that had reason to be in the courthouse. That meant guards would have nodded as the people passed by and might not have retained a memory of all of them, especially if they were distracted by someone less familiar. Nolan understood, even as it frustrated him. What he'd give to have camera footage of all entrances, at the very least.

Did he really think a local defense attorney or do-gooder involved in the juvenile diversion program was the bomber? No. But at this point, they couldn't afford to dismiss anyone.

After a woman who the detective appeared to know well walked out, Roanne blurted, "There's a third entrance into the courthouse. You may have noticed it—"

He refrained from swearing. "No."

She eyed him warily. "It's between the east wing and the courthouse. The prosecutors have their offices there, as does Child Protective Services."

"Is *that* door guarded?"

"Mostly?"

Now he did swear. "The west wing is the police department and the jail. Please tell me there isn't a welcome mat there as well."

"When the new police station was built, the decision was made to isolate it. It's a nuisance sometimes when it's rainy, but at least that's something we don't have to worry about."

They talked to a few more people. Could someone have been bribed to carry the package in? Conceivably, but Nolan leaned against the possibility. Corruption could be found anywhere, but unless he was being incredibly naive, it seemed less likely in a town the size of Rosendaal. It could have been an off-handed request for a favor…except who wouldn't have wondered at the sloppy wrappings and writing on the package? And once hearing about the bomb, that person would be sure to remember the odd package. He hadn't seen so much as a flicker of guilt on any face.

He'd have liked to dismiss his awareness of Roanne sitting barely a foot away from him but never quite managed. Nolan wondered if she had any idea of the expressiveness of her face. He hoped he would see if one of these witnesses, or the names they spouted, jarred her in some way but couldn't be sure.

The interviews ate up the entire afternoon. He'd think they must be done, look at a list and realize there was an entire department still to be summoned.

Roanne and he took only brief breaks. One would fetch the coffee, while—in his case, at least—the other stretched and walked around for a minute.

His head had begun to throb, and he could only imagine how Roanne felt. Shuffling through lists on his laptop, he said, "Why are there so many people missing?"

"Remember that flu I mentioned?"

"Oh." He gusted out a breath.

At a rap on the door, Nolan called, "Come in."

The police chief, a man who had to be approaching sixty but looked lean and fit, stepped in.

Roanne nodded. "Chief. Oh, Agent Cantrell, have you met Chief Brenk?"

"Briefly." Nolan stood so they could shake hands.

"Any progress?" the older man asked.

"About all we could expect at this point," Nolan said, watching for any even slightly off expression on the chief's face. "We have an extremely long list of people who entered the courthouse over the course of two days."

"You're not going further back than that?"

Roanne explained their reasoning, and her boss grimaced.

"That makes sense."

"Of course, now comes the hard work."

"Plus, we have to catch up with everyone who went out sick that day—or claimed to. They could have made a quick stop."

"Fire department has been hit hard, too," Brenk told them. "Several trials were postponed last week because of the flu."

"I suppose the schools have been hit as well."

"No chance you're looking for a teenager?"

Nolan didn't hesitate to say, "I think we can rule that out. This device was sophisticated enough, and planted cleverly enough, that I believe we're looking at an adult. The usual profile would suggest twenties to thirties, conceivably a bit older than that. And male."

The chief grunted. "Okay, what do you need from me? I can scrape up some manpower, but not a lot, not with tulip season almost on us coinciding with that damn flu."

Roanne reminded him about the accusation against the county councilman, and he promised to send someone else. He offered to loan them a couple of officers to check backgrounds on the names they'd gathered.

Nolan did pause at that, but there was only so much he and Roanne could accomplish on their own. He could probably co-opt a member of the NRT but trusted them to be researching any other bombs or bomb threats in the state.

"We didn't hunt down Billman yet," Roanne reminded him. "I can trace him from home tonight."

They threw around ideas, none of which were remotely useful, and agreed to at least take a break for dinner.

Chief Brenk left them after saying, "Call me anytime."

"Will do," Nolan agreed. Then he raised his brows at Roanne. "Your dad expecting you for dinner?"

"Well, I'm sure he'd feed me. Probably both of us, if you want to join me."

He shook his head. "I'd rather we eat in a quiet booth where we can talk without being overheard. Any suggestion?"

"Do you like Thai?"

"Sure." He shoved back his chair, rose to his feet and groaned. "I'll drive."

She showed a flash of wariness. "But..."

"Your car has sat out front all day again. Call me paranoid. We'll need somebody to look at it again, probably in the morning. No point in following each other anyway."

"I suppose not." She stood more slowly than he had, undoubtedly feeling every wrenched muscle, bruised hip and shoulder, and tear in her smooth skin from the shrapnel.

"At least I didn't get sick," she mumbled.

He grinned at her. "A woman who appreciates silver linings."

Roanne rolled her eyes. "That's me. Little Miss Sunshine."

"Are you better known as the crank down at the station?"

She laughed. "No, I'm easygoing. Just...feeling the past few days. I hate sitting for hours."

"Me, too."

Both packed up their laptops along with lined pads of paper where they'd scrawled notes.

She showed him the door in the basement that led to the east wing, which indeed had a guard stationed on this side. He introduced himself as Wade Jordan. Roanne didn't appear to know him, which made Nolan nervous.

She was the one to ask him for his recollections of traffic through this entrance, and she and Nolan waited as the guard's forehead creased in deep thought. He finally named several attorneys. Roanne thanked him but hadn't yet turned away when he said, "Oh, we had some maintenance. Almost forgot them."

"Maintenance." Nolan tried to keep any inflection out of his voice while refraining from gritting his teeth.

"Pipe overflowed here in the basement the night before. They wanted to be sure there wasn't any leakage over here in the courthouse."

He offered a list of names, which Roanne accepted from him.

As she and Nolan turned away, the guard spoke to their backs. "Almost forgot. The office-equipment repair guy was here, too. We've had a contract with him for... what? A year?"

"Him?"

"It's the only company in town that repairs copiers and what have you. I think he bought it from Ed Carlan. Guy's here every week or two. Brown uniform?"

"I've seen him," Roanne agreed. "We'll get in touch with him."

Nolan growled, but she ignored him, instead calling her father to let him know she wouldn't join him for dinner.

Her dad said something Nolan couldn't make out.

Her gaze slid sidelong. "Honestly, I think I'd like to sleep in my own bed. I'm a lot more clear-headed than I was yesterday. Agent Cantrell will drop me off, since my car has been sitting out on the street unsupervised all day." She listened. "That's unlikely, but he seems determined to be cautious....Really. Don't worry, Dad. How about if I give you a call in the morning before we go back to work?"

After she put away her phone, they made their way in silence out to his vehicle. Nolan resisted the renewed urge to give her a boost up onto the passenger seat.

Once they were in, he said, "I'll need directions."

They were brief, and he recalled noting the restaurant when he first drove into town.

"I don't usually let my father fuss like that," Roanne said as he was turning onto the street.

So she'd read his mind. "I understand why you moved back to town and why you're being so patient," he said, knowing he'd shoot himself if he had his own father hanging over his shoulder. To the distress of his mother, he and Dad had clashed from the time Nolan was around ten years old. Even now, Nolan wasn't sure what had happened. If Mom had stood up for him, it might have been different, but the distance that had inevitably opened between himself and his parents could explain why he had trouble imagining the intimacy he'd have to share with a woman. Especially if they were promising each other a lifetime.

"What about your family?" Roanne asked tentatively.

"I go home for holidays, but I'm not close to them. They retired over on Bainbridge Island," he added. "Great views, and a quick ferry ride when they want civilization."

"That sounds lovely. Not practical for either of us, though."

"No." There were days when he thought about walking on the rocky beach, maybe settling against a driftwood log to nap when the sun was out. Unfortunately, he was almost always immersed in an investigation—or in several, including those he supervised. When that was the case, he wasn't good at taking time off. His workaholic tendencies were built upon the fact that he was thirty-six years old and never had been in a lasting relationship. Or was the choice to prioritize work deliberate, if only on a subconscious level? Good excuse to ensure he never really trusted a woman enough to imagine anything as permanent as marriage.

Even as he parked outside the restaurant, Nolan wondered why his thoughts had wandered the way they had. It wasn't like him. Maybe it had to do with his dislike of the controlling man his sister had married.

Nolan's mind took another, unexpected hop. Would *he* appear controlling to someone looking from the outside in? Someone like Detective Roanne Engle?

Surely it wasn't this woman he'd known for two days who was responsible for his ruminations?

They walked in together, let the hostess seat them at a booth in a far corner and even made small talk while he browsed the menu. Below the surface, his self-analysis continued.

Not controlling, he decided. That wasn't his flaw. He just tended to forget anyone and everything else once his attention locked onto his job.

Which was a good reason not to succumb to temptation where the woman studying him from across the table was concerned. She looked wary again. *Smart*, he thought.

Chapter Six

Gaze resting on her, Agent Cantrell reached for a spring roll.

As aware as he must've been of the party of fellow diners lingering at the booth behind her, Roanne postponed jumping back into the investigation, even though she was better at that kind of conversation than she was at dating chitchat. Which, despite that they weren't dating, was about all she could come up with.

Dipping her own spring roll into sauce, she asked, "Did you apply to the FBI right out of the army?"

His eyes flicked to someone who spoke out especially loudly just past her shoulder, but he dismissed them. "No, the FBI requires more qualifications than just having served. I had a college degree, but when I said *thanks, no thanks* to the ATF, I went to law school. Never intended to practice. By that time, I had my eye on the agency. I don't love sitting behind a desk for long. I'm restless."

"I guess I am, too," she admitted. "I majored in sociology, but I took a criminology class my sophomore year and got hooked. Without really articulating it, I thought maybe I could balance some of the bad stuff happening, like the drunk driver killing my brother, with helping others." She made a face. "Turns out what any of us can do is a drop in the bucket, but... I've mostly been satisfied."

He nodded. "A certain amount of resignation is inevitable, and some cops seem able to let the bad stuff go. On the other hand, I've met detectives teetering on the edge of retirement who mostly are holding on because of a single case that went cold years before that they can't give up on."

"I can see that." Just refusing to give up. That would be her.

What would happen if the bomber they sought never set another device? If they never figured this out? They could both live with it because nobody had been killed, but if somebody had been blown to bits, it would be hard to let go. And even now...the prickly awareness of her surroundings that he urged on her would be hard to sustain. One day would she just decide to assume there'd be no repeat, shrug and go on her way?

"Anybody tackling cold cases locally?" Nolan asked.

"Not really. I've dragged a couple out but not gotten anywhere. A girl I knew in middle school was raped and killed. It was probably the worst crime committed in Rosendaal in the past half century. I think about that one sometimes at night."

"Any DNA evidence that can be traced?"

"You mean with the genealogy websites?"

"Every day or two, I catch a headline about victims and killers from thirty years ago being identified."

Despite her frustration, Roanne understood the roadblocks. "Chief Brenk doesn't have the money to pay for the forensic genealogy, and we don't have anyone in the department with that kind of expertise."

"There are foundations that sometimes fund a search

like that," he told her. "Tell me more about it later, and I may have an idea."

"Really?" She tried not to believe too much in hope that was so ephemeral but couldn't help herself. Nolan Cantrell worked for the FBI and, from what she'd gathered, had gained enough seniority—or maybe it was success—to be in a supervisory position. Despite what a short time she'd known him, she believed he'd do what he said. "I'll hold you to that." She beamed at him.

The group behind them left at last, still talking loudly, so Roanne and Nolan finally had some privacy. He shared some frustration because they had so little to go on and so many possibilities but conceded that was often the case when an investigation first opened.

"This one is especially disturbing, though," he said. "The intended victim is well-liked and in a long career has presided over a staggering number of trials." His shoulders jerked. "So far, I haven't so much as seen a string to pull."

"No." She pressed her lips together. "Oh, that's not true. Don't forget Andrew Billman. Nailing down his whereabouts is rising to the top of my to-do list."

"Do you see him as someone capable of putting together a fairly intricate explosive device?"

"I don't know," Roanne said slowly, thinking about it. "He was hot-tempered—I remember that, but does that mean he can't patiently plot revenge?"

"What did he do for a living?"

"He was an electrician."

Agent Cantrell's eyebrow crooked. "Which means he understands wires better than you do?"

She refrained from sticking her tongue out at an FBI agent—that couldn't possibly be professional—but let herself laugh. "That's a low blow."

Damn. She wished he wouldn't smile at her like that. The skin beside his eyes crinkled, and the slight twitches of his lips made her extremely aware of how sexy his mouth was, never mind the penetrating gaze.

"Couldn't resist." He stretched and said, "We can potentially get more done tonight. Talk our way through that never-ending list, if nothing else. I'd like to hear your gut feelings about people you know."

"Agent Cantrell..."

There went that eyebrow again. "We've spent enough time together—I think we can be on a first-name basis."

"Fine. You're welcome to come back to my place with me, if you'd like, or we can sit down at your hotel if your room has a table and chairs."

"No, it's bare bones. Crappy mattress, too."

"I admit I haven't heard good things about the place. We've made some arrests there. Drug deals." She shrugged. "Prostitution."

"At least it's clean. Still, if I'm going to stay locally, I may look for someplace else."

Anxiety widened her eyes. "You don't expect to be here long?"

"Depends. What if a similar bomb is set off in Everett or Bellingham? We can't be positive our guy is local."

"Andrew Billman wasn't," she said. "I think he lived in Marysville. Snohomish County."

"Right now, I don't plan to go anywhere except your place, assuming you're not uncomfortable with that."

Roanne summoned what she hoped was a poised smile to suggest she hadn't the slightest qualm at the thought of having him in her small house. Well, she didn't, not in the sense she was afraid of him.

More of herself. Except nothing would come of that.

Aside from a few glints in his blue eyes, she had no reason to think he even thought of her as a woman versus a detective employed by small city in a primarily rural county. Right now, he had a use for her, but that didn't mean he'd signed on to be her partner for the weeks to come.

"Of course I'm not!" she insisted. "It makes sense to huddle around my kitchen table. At least we can't be overheard."

"Good," he said, sliding from the booth then waiting for her to do the same. "I'd like to see your place anyway. Make a risk assessment."

Oh, wasn't that comforting.

"You're taking quite a leap to think he'd bother coming after me. I mean, it could have been *anyone* who interceded."

"But it wasn't," he said, his expression closed.

She wasn't about to argue. To date, she hadn't worried much about home security. She slept with her sidearm in her bedside table. Neighbors certainly knew she was a cop. If the bomber had learned her name, he too would know she was law enforcement. Not a house you wanted to break into.

As they left the restaurant and crossed the dark parking lot, Roanne saw the man beside her turning his head and evaluating their surroundings, his face hard again. Yep, Special Agent Nolan Cantrell had reemerged…assuming he'd set aside that part of himself even for a second while they chatted.

She shouldn't let herself be so fascinated by someone whose path was crossing hers so briefly.

Her home had been built in the 1940s and boasted a broad front porch, two small bedrooms with dormers upstairs and a detached garage.

"I wish that was attached," he said, parking in the driveway.

Of course, he was frowning at the garage.

"I do sometimes, too, but there's no easy answer. I haven't felt unsafe at home."

Until now, Roanne thought, aware again of her sense that Nolan was hearing every sound within a block, at least, seeing the neighbor's cat darting under a lilac bush, a baby crying two doors down. She was glad to usher him inside, locking the door behind them.

She was never exactly messy, but she was glad she'd left the house tidier than sometimes yesterday. In the kitchen, she said, "Will this work?" and closed the blinds over the sink when he pulled out a chair at the small table and sat down.

Roanne made coffee, and they dove right into the endless list they'd compiled today. She knew quite a few people on it well enough to confidently eliminate them. Nolan challenged her about a couple, nodding when she explained what she was thinking.

They divided up the other names and searched online, quiet in their concentration. She had friends who dropped by sometimes, but this felt different. He'd move a little— roll his shoulders, knead the back of his neck. The chair would creak, and she'd feel instant, prickly awareness of how much bigger he was than any of the few men she considered friends, of how he radiated intensity. Occasionally she'd catch herself watching his hands on his keyboard, bones and tendons standing out, a few small hairs curling on the backs of fingers. Or noticing how muscular his forearms were, how thick his wrists compared to hers.

She liked to think she had outgrown blushing but saw

an occasional quirk of his mouth that made her suspect he'd noticed her wandering attention.

"Billman," he said suddenly, "is apparently a resident in the Snohomish County jail and has been for thirty days. Beat the crap out of a guy at a tavern. He's skipped some required counseling from a previous conviction, too, so he's facing serious assault charges."

"We'll have to verify in the morning."

Nolan grunted.

They worked for what had to be three hours. He took a couple of calls, both times walking out on her front porch, presumably so she couldn't hear the conversations. Or was she unfairly suspicious? He might've been trying to avoid distracting her.

The second time, she glanced at him when he returned to the kitchen, lines furrowed more deeply on his forehead. She raised her eyebrows, and he said, "Donahue has come up with half a dozen other incidents of explosive devices in the past year in western Washington. Sounds like most were designed to set a fire rather than injure someone, but he's going to pursue those further tomorrow."

"I remember a couple of arson fires in Everett," she agreed. "Couldn't you put together something pretty simple just to create a flame that would have time to spread?"

"It's true, those are often more primitive." He still looked disturbed. "Sometimes a wildfire arsonist will get fancier. Or is there any chance Judge Anderson presided over a trial involved in one or more of these suspects?"

"Assuming someone was arrested, I guess so, but not for a crime committed in Snohomish County."

He let out a breath and returned his attention to his laptop, leaving her to do the same.

She was unsettled enough by the unexpected background of a court commissioner, a man whose name was vaguely familiar to her but whose face she couldn't picture, that it took a moment for her to notice the clicking across the table had stopped. Roanne looked up to find him studying her.

"You take anything recently for that headache?" he asked.

She'd never in her life been monitored so closely.

"My headache has been creeping back on me," she admitted. "I wish I had a hot tub or a Jacuzzi."

"If you belong to a health club, you could take time for one tomorrow."

"I do, but I don't make it there as often as I should. Once I've worked out, it feels too lazy to soak in the hot tub."

"Take something for the headache. We also need to get some sleep."

"Yeah, okay." Roanne had been carrying a prescription painkiller around in her handbag and swallowed two pills with a glass of water at the sink. She couldn't see out with the blinds down but wondered with a tiny prickle of disquiet whether from the outside, her silhouette would be visible to a watcher out there in her yard.

She gave fleeting thought to walking a perimeter after Nolan left, but why would someone be watching her house?

By the time she turned back, Nolan had zipped his laptop inside his case and was pushing back his chair.

"I wish you had a roommate," he startled her by saying. "Or would stay at your dad's house for a few days."

She stiffened. "Really? If I were a man, would that have even occurred to you?"

"Under these circumstances, it might." He shook his head. "Occupational paranoia."

Roanne wanted to ask if he was married or had kids and whether, if so, he lived on a knife-edge of anxiety for them, but of course that wasn't any of her business.

"You'll pick me up in the morning?" She really needed to reclaim her own car.

"Yeah. Eight?"

"Works for me."

COME MORNING, SHE and Nolan no sooner had entered the courthouse than a clerk called, "Detective Engle? The chief wants to see you."

Roanne waved back.

"He'd better not have decided he can't afford to have you sidetracked like this," Nolan growled.

"That's possible. I mean, we don't have the manpower you're probably used to being able to draw on. He may just want an update, though. I'm surprised he hasn't tried to jump into the investigation."

"God save me from unwanted help."

Looking at his tight lips, she decided she could take that as an accolade, she being so useful. "Are we meeting at the same time upstairs? I'd better talk to Chief Brenk, and then I'll join you."

They'd reached the elevator. Nolan stopped her with a hand on her arm. "I shouldn't have said that."

"About Chief Brenk? My lips are sealed." She pretended to zip them. "I'm sure wherever you go, you end up tripping over a bunch of eager volunteers that you're too nice to dismiss."

Nolan flashed an irresistible grin. "That's me. Mr. Nice-Guy."

"If you weren't nice, you wouldn't have sat by my hospital bedside all night, reassured me after nightmares, reminded me how to increase my pain meds. Just...making sure I didn't feel alone."

He silently gazed down at her for long enough to have her wishing she'd kept her big mouth shut.

Then he nodded and pushed the elevator button. "Join us as soon as you can."

The police department was situated in the west wing, a modern building attached to the courthouse. A door connecting the two buildings would have been convenient given the rainfall in Washington state, but she was grateful now about the decision because of this investigation.

She smiled at the receptionist, who waved her back. A light rap on the chief's door and he called, "Come in." When he saw her, he added, "Have a seat."

Sure enough, he mostly wanted to find out whether all those federal agents working around the clock had come up with anything. "They're the experts."

"I've been working long days, too, and I've got to tell you, unless the ATF agent comes up with something that was careless or too distinctive, it's not going to be easy. I think..." She hesitated. "We're all expecting another bomb. Maybe one that fails to go off, taking the guesswork out of analyzing the construction—and making it likelier that we'll find fingerprints or DNA."

He grunted. "We're stuck with the pack of wolves I'm sure will be just what we need."

Shortly thereafter, he waved her off to attend the morning meeting in conference room C, where she learned next to nothing and found herself zoning out often enough she hoped nobody was noticing.

Catching her attention, one of the ATF agents said,

"Question is was Judge Anderson a priority or only handy for a first attempt given the abysmal lack of security at the courthouse? Or was he the brass ring, the victim our bomber has dreamed the longest of killing?"

Agent Kroger raised her eyebrows. "If that's the case, wouldn't you think the best would be saved for last?"

"Unless other projected victims are trickier to get to. Or our guy knows that other victims could help us narrow down the aggrieved perpetrator. A superior court judge? Lots of people are bound to hate him." Nolan shrugged. "This way, the mystery plays out longer, whereas with some victims, he'd be as good as waving a red flag to say, *We all know what their one glaring offense was.*"

The quiet lasted longer than most given this crowd.

Nobody looked at Roanne, but she couldn't help thinking, *Everyone does know what* my *offense was*. Her nape tingled, as if somebody had tiptoed up behind her and breathed down her neck.

NOLAN WISHED ROANNE hadn't been a heroine, just a woman who attracted him but hadn't placed herself smack dab in the middle of this investigation. The bomber had to be ticked that she had not only thwarted his first grand assault but was also universally admired.

He wasn't surprised to receive a call from John Mitchell, who had accepted the role of finding housing and conference space for the enlarged FBI troops. Since the city had offered ideal conference space, John was stuck grumbling about where agents were supposed to lay their heads at night.

"All we need is one hotel to cancel their reservations. We can pay them off."

"Then what?" Nolan asked. "I understand the problem,

but can we cut checks for every restaurant in town that depends on tourist traffic? Every gift shop losing business? Anyplace where tourists usually buy posters and postcards, T-shirts, cute ceramics. Tour bus business—"

John sighed. "I tried neighboring communities, but guess what?"

"Their economies depend on the tulip festival," Nolan said with resignation. "What about Everett?"

"Too long a drive."

"Detective Engle thought some townspeople would open their homes and let an agent or two have a guest room."

John grunted. "You tested the idea?"

"Her father has two spare bedrooms, and she feels sure he'd welcome the company."

"Lonely, is he?"

"It's not ideal," Nolan admitted.

"You have a room with two queen-size beds. I can stick someone else in with you."

Oh, yeah, that would be fun. "I may have an alternative." He slid a glance sideways, meeting narrowed eyes. The hell anyone else would move in with Roanne.

Chapter Seven

Headache lingering and eyes feeling grainy, Roanne all but stomped out to the curb in front of her house, where her garbage can lay on its side, spilling several white bags of kitchen trash, as well as some personal products from the bathroom that she'd rather not be displayed to the whole neighborhood.

This was why she attached a stretchy cord with a hook on each end over the lid of the blasted can. She *knew* she'd done it last night. It was habit.

Now she'd be late to morning meeting, not that any of them had learned anything worth sharing in the past couple of days. Still, it didn't look good.

Something was oozing out of one of the white bags onto the sidewalk. Aging mayonnaise. Oh, ick. She'd need to grab some gloves before she cleaned up— In the act of turning away from the mess, Roanne froze. Her heartbeat picked up speed.

Nolan's grim words played back for her.

I need you to take my concerns seriously, too. Do you understand me? Don't go for walks. Don't open a door or window without studying it carefully. Not a move you make can be unthinking, casual.

Oh, God. Was this a *setup*?

She kept breathing but otherwise stayed light on the balls of her feet, unmoving. She had to turn her head to see the disaster: the plastic can dented on one side as if someone had kicked it; the heap of several still-closed bags, the couple that had either split open or had been sliced open.

Was there a wire anywhere?

Suddenly lightheaded, Roanne realized she might not have been breathing after all.

Step backward, she decided, and did. One cautious foot after another. And was that the distant squeal of the brakes on the garbage pickup truck? A few blocks away, but...

Pride reared its head. Maybe she could go fetch a brick and from a safe distance away, throw it had the spilled garbage. It would either go *Boom!*—or nothing would happen and she could pick up the mess and get to work.

With a sigh, she backed up almost to her front porch and took out her phone.

Nolan answered sharply, "Roanne?"

"I think I'm being super suspicious, but, um, last night I put out my garbage can for pickup. I'm always neat, and I stretched a strap across the lid so even if the can falls over, the lid will stay on."

Paranoid might have been a better word. She couldn't take her gaze from the sprawl of garbage on her stretch of the sidewalk.

"I'm on my way," he snapped. "You haven't touched anything, have you?"

"No."

"Don't!"

Indignant, she opened her mouth to retort but then realized the line was dead.

A garage door clanked, then rose slowly, right across

the street. One of Roanne's neighbors backed out in his Ford F-250, reached the street and braked. A remodeling contractor, in the bed of his truck he carried a ladder, shiny silver toolbox, piles of lumber and she thought some Sheetrock.

Even as he used the remote to set his garage to closing again, Don Kinney hopped out and started across the street to her.

"Not my favorite sight in the morning," he called. "Let me give you a hand. Suppose it was those raccoons again?"

She got over her paralysis in time to cut him off midstreet. "Thanks for the offer, but, uh, I've got someone coming to take a look at it before I clean up. I don't think this was wildlife. It looks an awful lot to me like someone knocked this over on purpose, and, well, I've had an eventful week."

His stare swung back to the spilled garbage. "Oh, yeah. I've been following the news. I thought you'd need time off, but you're heading that investigation?"

Time to hide her damaged wrist again. "My injuries weren't that serious."

Tires squealed down the block, and she immediately recognized Nolan's big black SUV. He swung to the curb a safe distance away, then leaped out and advanced on her.

"Don here was just reminding me what a time we had with a pair of young racoons a year or two ago. It could be…" She trailed off, given that he was studying the modest pile of garbage with narrowed eyes. He all but vibrated with intensity.

"I'm sorry if I've wasted your time."

All the intensity in that gaze came to bear on her face.

"I'd be really, really mad at you if you'd gotten yourself blown up this morning."

"I guess I wouldn't care, though, would I?" She smiled weakly.

He was not amused.

Ignoring her, he asked her neighbor if he'd heard any noise out here earlier and if he'd happened to glance out at any time and noticed the mess.

"Afraid not." Don shook his head. "I gave Melly her bottle at around two thirty, then crashed. We can ask Robin—my wife—she was up at six or six thirty."

"I'll do that," Nolan said. "You may as well get on to work. We're going to have to sift through this pile one shred at a time."

Roanne's neighbor looked at her in alarm. "You'll be doing that?"

"No. We have some experts from the Bureau of Alcohol, Firearms, Tobacco and Arson in town, and they're know how to do it without any oops moments."

With a last disturbed glance over his shoulder, Don drove away down the street.

Roanne made herself meet Nolan's eyes. "Before you ask, no, I didn't hear a thing during the night."

"You taking pain meds and sleeping more soundly than usual?" he asked.

"Sometimes. Sometimes I have trouble staying asleep. This—" she gestured "—could have been done without a lot of racket. If my can had been metal, it may have been different."

She heard a buzz, and he glanced down at his phone hanging from his belt.

"Crew is on the way. I'm inclined to divert the garbage truck back at the corner. Better safe than sorry."

"Everybody in town will be freaked."

"I hope they are," Nolan said grimly.

In the end, they sat on porch steps watching as the ATF group suited up for bomb disposal sifted through her garbage. It was surreal, sitting here watching, thankful she hadn't dumped something really embarrassing in her garbage.

What would that be? She couldn't think of anything. If there'd been some used condoms, she'd have been embarrassed, but nobody else would think twice about it. Strange thoughts bouncing in her head like pucks careening off the wall of a hockey arena, it occurred to her she'd felt more emotions this week than she had in a month or more.

Maybe she had let herself stultify. Maybe she should go wild.

Roanne made a sound that made Nolan turn his head to focus on her face. The sad thing was she couldn't think of anything wild to do that sounded the least bit exciting, except maybe inviting a particular FBI agent to share her bed.

NOLAN WANTED TO be doing something more useful than watch from a distance as his colleagues worked in their methodical, even prissy, way. As it was, he kept being distracted by fleeting emotions crossing Roanne's face. Nothing he could pin down.

Damn it, he didn't want her staying in this house alone, but he didn't like the idea of her putting up at her father's house, either. Maybe he'd reserve the room right beside his at the Tulip Inn. Because he could watch over her with X-ray vision, when he wasn't imagining being in bed with her.

And yeah, she'd be pissed if she could read his mind. No, he wasn't worrying the same way about any of his other team members.

Sharon Krogen reared up from her original crouch in the middle of the sliced open trash bags, her voice sounding hollow from inside the head covering. "What the...?"

The others crowded closer. Nolan didn't object when Roanne joined him at the sidewalk.

A cracked toy water pistol lay amid a tangle of wires. Short ones, as if someone had stripped the paper part off the ones shoppers grabbed in the grocery store produce department to close bags. It mostly just looked weird... except for a torn piece of lined paper that had big letters in red marker.

THE NEXT BIG BANG COULD HAPPEN ANYWHERE. ANYTIME.

"A lot of trouble to send a message," Sharon said thoughtfully. "Why does he want to play with you?"

Roanne gaped. "I have no idea."

Nolan's jaws ground together. "I'll be really surprised if you don't know this guy."

"Oh, yeah," ATF Agent Castanares agreed.

"Does this suggest anything to you?" Nolan asked Roanne.

She shook her head. "Nothing."

"The TV show?"

Her shoulders hunched. "Who hasn't watched *The Big Bang Theory*?"

Nobody present raised a hand.

Nolan sighed and said, "How about we talk before we go our own ways?"

They would have to canvass Roanne's neighborhood in hopes of some miraculous, middle-of-the-night sighting.

Nolan made a note to call Judge Anderson and reiterate his cautions. He hadn't seemed interested in packing up his wife for a two-week vacation, but having this occur in front of Roanne's house might give him second thoughts.

"I'd like your father to go somewhere, too," he said, catching surprise on several faces. He'd apparently tuned out briefly. "This is too personal. Serial bombings usually have a point. A political cause. Getting even with someone. Rage, obsession. He's undoubtedly planning other bombings, so why hasn't he moved onto that instead of taking a chance of being seen just so he could enjoy scaring you?"

They all seemed to be watching Roanne now, if cautiously. Was he supposed to be the one to speak up and say, *I'm tossing you off this team for your own good?*

He would in a heartbeat, if he thought she'd accept the dismissal. If he could have interviewed her and left her out of the investigation from the beginning, that might have been smart. His gut said it was too late now.

Anyway, what they'd just learned only reinforced the belief the bomber was very much a local boy. He was betting that Roanne was smarter than their nemesis, who wouldn't understand how much he gave away with every bomb set, every message sent.

Nolan and Roanne started with the door-knocking. She stayed on her side of the street while he took the opposite. They went up and down cross streets, too, and given that the homeowner right behind her house wasn't there right now, Nolan and Roanne trotted across the ragged lawn to inspect her fence.

"I knew those dandelions must have been coming from here," she grumbled.

"They're kind of pretty."

She just looked at him.

Hardly anyone was home; most of the small houses either were rentals or owned by young couples, people who'd left for work.

"I'll knock on some doors again tonight," Roanne said.

Nolan kept his mouth shut. She wouldn't be staying in her home tonight if he had anything to say about it. She certainly wouldn't be wandering up and down dark sidewalks on her own.

He was increasingly annoyed at himself by this over-the-top need to protect her. He'd served with female soldiers in the army. His best friend from law school was a woman, and the ranks of the FBI had swelled with female rookies as well as male ones. Well, he also couldn't remember partnering with anyone on an investigation when that partner wore a bull's eye.

When they reached the main group in front of her garage, Roanne said, "I had a thought during the night. I haven't paid that much attention to your parts list, but just a few weeks ago, the school district maintenance barn had a break-in. I wasn't primary, so I can't tell you exactly what was taken, but there are six schools in our district and I have no idea how many buses running every day. If you're looking for plumbing or hardware or maybe even gasoline or explosives, that may have been like an open house to a bomber who had all night long to pick and choose."

A profanity crossed his lips. "Why did nobody think to say?"

"I'm sorry—it just came to me."

"I wasn't complaining about you," Nolan grumbled. "Don't suppose any suspects were identified?"

"I don't think so, but we can find out whether security cameras caught anything. It seems to me that mostly there was relief nobody had driven off with a bulldozer or a school bus then wrecked it."

Nolan winced at the memory of a school bus heist a couple of years ago. Up on the northwest coast of the state, a dangerously curvy road had been built to hug the sheer sandstone cliffs of the Chuckanut Mountains. The only place where the Cascade Mountains met the sea, the scenic drive overlooked Samish Bay and the San Juan Islands and Chuckanut Bay.

In that tragic case, two drunk high school boys had driven off a cliff. Their bodies had been recovered from the tumultuous sea the next day, while the bus, broken into dozens of pieces, had been salvaged over the course of months.

No surprise the local school officials had been relieved rather than especially alarmed by the recent break-in. Nolan felt confident that spare parts walked their way out of the maintenance building all the time anyway. If it was the last thing he'd do, he would convince these people that improved security could, in fact, reduce crime and save lives.

Roanne stood looking at her house. "I wonder how soon I could have some security cameras installed here."

"Quick, I'll bet, but I'm going to suggest you hire an out-of-town company to do it. You could feel more confident in the integrity of the work."

She shuddered. "I've always liked my job, but I really hate this constant, creepy feeling that someone could be watching, planning, aiming at *me*."

"I understand." He, too, felt the uneasy sensation that malevolent eyes might be watching them, listening in, even participating in some of the alarmed community meetings.

Why not have built a real device to tear Detective Engle's garbage and possibly her to smithereens? Because the bomber would be annoyed if he blew up the garbage collector?

The note suggested otherwise.

So, why a taunt?

Nolan wanted to believe this meant she wasn't a real target. The bomber hadn't wanted to waste a device on her, just scare her a little because she'd gotten in his way.

He wished he felt more confident that she really was peripheral and not a primary target.

911 OPERATOR: *"YOU THINK you need an ambulance. Are you hurt?"*

"No!" Even shrieking, the voice was obviously a child's. "It's Daddy. He isn't getting up. I'm scared."

911 operator: *"Did he fall? Did he ask you to call?"*

"No! Will you please come? Daddy is all bloody and..." Hiccup. "I don't know. I heard a *boom*."

Somehow, the dispatcher managed to stay calm, telling the child an EMS unit was on the way to take care of the child's father. *"Please let them in when they arrive."*

"He's on the porch." The child's voice hitched. "Except the porch is...not really there."

NOLAN'S SUV ROCKETED down the residential street, faster than was safe. He wished that Roanne was with him, but by the time he'd called, she, too, had already listened to the blood-chilling 911 message and was on her way across town. If the purpose had been to lure her...

He growled and gave himself a lecture that didn't take.

As he neared the address, he noted that the houses in this neighborhood mostly dated to the same era as her home and had detached garages but were much larger and sat on substantial lots. The address was only three blocks from her dad's house.

Even before he took in the devastation, Nolan scanned for Roanne. Amid the crowd of first responders, including a couple of ATF team members...no, there she was. Her head turned before he pulled up to the curb, and when she spotted him, she didn't look away until he'd leaped out of his vehicle and joined her on the sidewalk in front of what had been a nice house. Big trees casting shade on a neat lawn, flower beds to each side of what had been the porch.

"It's really ugly," Roanne said quietly. "Worse than I imagined from the 911 recording. That poor kid."

Yeah, the way she'd wailed at the end had him clenching his teeth. He sought out the child and realized a firefighter had scooped her up and carried her a distance from the ruined porch and the mangled body sprawled amid the debris. Given the extensive damage, the dead man's identity would need to be confirmed by the medical examiner.

"You know the residents?" he asked.

"I know the little girl's father." With desperation and grief in her eyes, she looked at Nolan. "The homeowner's name is Curtis Whitley. I can't remember what his wife's name is, but he mentioned her sometimes." She drew a deep breath. "He's a prosecutor."

"At least something ties the victims together," he growled.

Vehicles with flashing lights lined both sides of the street on this block. ATF and police jackets and T-shirts crowded the scene. A second fire truck braked in the middle of the street. Sharon and a couple of teammates had roped off the crime scene and snapped at anyone whose booted foot ventured too close to the tape, even if they were aiming a stream from a hose to prevent the spread of fire.

Roanne's stare was fixed on the body. "Yes, but remember what a small town this is. You could probably tie any two people together, with a little effort." Okay, that was weak, but...

She didn't argue when he cocked a skeptical brow at her.

What had been a wide porch that must have accented the handsome house might as well be construction debris. Part of the roof dangled, the support post lying to one side. The front of the house was blackened but wet from a stream of water shot out of a hose. Sharon was arguing with a red-faced firefighter that the water be turned off.

Heaps of splintered wood lay on the lawn and buried a flower bed.

Two EMTs crouched beside the body that lay amid the destruction. The lack of urgency told Nolan that Curtis Whitley was dead, not that he'd had any doubt.

"Has anybody tracked down her mother?" Roanne said. "And I think there may have been a younger kid, a boy, like three or four?"

He looked up at the windows, some shattered, some intact. Where *were* the mother and the other kid? And how had this girl escaped the impact of the bomb?

Roanne took off down the sidewalk, aiming for the girl. Nolan let out an expletive and chased after her. She dropped to her knees in front of the child. "Oh, sweetheart."

The girl's face was streaked with blood, her hair a mess tangled with soot. Roanne hugged the shell-shocked child who looked to be about seven or eight. The officer who had been shielding her from the devastation backed away, expression relieved.

The girl's face tipped up to her. "Can they fix Daddy?"

Nolan could tell Roanne wanted to lie. *He* wanted to lie. She said softly, "I don't know for sure yet. But... I don't think so. I'm so sorry, honey, but I think he's dead."

Neither of them said a word for several minutes.

"My cat died," the child said matter-of-factly. "We buried him in the backyard. So...so he wouldn't miss us."

Tears streaking Roanne's face, she asked, "Do you know where your mommy is?"

Now sobbing, she said, "I... I don't know for sure. I think she's at work."

"And your brother?"

"Mommy always took him to his daycare. Daddy and I were going to do something fun, except I don't know what it was going to be. Daddy likes to surprise me." Her face crumpled.

"Oh, sweetheart," Roanne said again and wrapped the girl in her arms.

A cop Nolan didn't recognize separated himself from a cluster and walked toward them. His gaze touched briefly on the little girl before he winced away from her.

"My partner knows the family. She's, uh, gone to pick up Mrs. Whitley at the elementary school."

"Oh, thank you!" Roanne exclaimed. "I'll stay with her until her mom arrives. I wish we could move the body before she gets here, but I suppose..."

Both men looked at her almost pityingly. Sure, that was going to happen.

"I'm so glad you weren't with your daddy," Roanne murmured.

Tear-wet eyes met hers. "I forgot my sweatshirt. Daddy said he'd wait. Only...only..."

"Your daddy would be so glad you did have to go back and weren't with him."

The girl, whose name Nolan had yet to hear, began to sob.

Chapter Eight

"Why don't people listen to us?" Sharon Krogen asked. Begged.

The usual morning meeting was taking place several hours later on the sidewalk half a block from the damaged home. They'd expected this, yes, but the surroundings were small-town America...and the bomber couldn't have known that he wasn't going to kill children. Or, almost as bad, the mother of young children.

"You're sure it wasn't a trip wire," ATF Agent Castanares said.

"Yes. I think an Amazon box, face down. Not that I've found so much as a scrap from a label. The original labels have to have been torn off."

Nolan could see it. Who didn't get regular shipments from the commerce giant, with their distinctive packaging? Even if Curtis Whitley hadn't ordered anything recently, he'd have figured his wife had.

Roanne and Nolan had spoken briefly to the wife, who was too distraught to interview more thoroughly. They'd determined that she wasn't aware her husband had been threatened, that she hadn't ordered anything from any online store in the past month and that Curtis and she had discussed safeguards.

"We did," she cried. "Especially where the kids are concerned! They know they aren't even to open the door to go out in the backyard without one of us. Carl loves his swing set and slide, so we constantly have to let him out." She seemed to be struck at that moment that there would be no more "we." Sobbing, she ran to rejoin her children on the lawn between houses, where they wouldn't have to look at Curtis's body or the damage to the house.

"The bastard could have rigged the swing set."

Shocked, Roanne said, "We have no reason to think he's targeting children!"

"No?" Nolan's blue eyes made her think of ice. "He had to have foreseen the possibility that either parent would have a kid with them when they left the house."

Distressed, she couldn't argue. "And so far, we haven't learned anything new."

"Give Sharon time. For now, we need to start canvassing and come back this evening to catch any neighbors who are at work."

Nobody answered the door at many of the houses within the surrounding blocks. People who were home had heard the explosion and were wide-eyed and frightened. None had happened to be out grabbing a newspaper from the front porch or even casually glancing out to note any passing traffic. Only one had seen Mrs. Whitley on her way to work and thought vaguely that she was running a little late. Pinned down, she said, "Like eight forty? Usually when I see her pass, it's more like eight thirty." Unfortunately, the witness had headed to the back of her house to throw in a load of laundry, then start dinner in a Crock-Pot.

Nobody else presently home had noticed their neighbor leaving for work.

Now, in the informal meeting on the sidewalk, Roanne said, "At least we have a time frame. A narrow one, at that."

One of the ATF agents grunted. "Which would be great if our guy had driven up in front, leaped out and set down his package as if he was a regular delivery driver. As it is, he could have been standing behind those lilac shrubs—" there was a hedge of them in fragrant bloom "—waiting for the wife to get out of there and Whitley to follow."

"And that means he knew their schedule," Nolan pointed out. "He's been watching them."

That struck Roanne as even more horrifying than the idea of a drive-by bombing, which was less...personal.

The first responder, a young RPD officer named Lee Gibson, said, "I sent my partner to circle the house and make sure no one was hanging around to watch the show."

"Good thinking," Roanne said, and others nodded. The trouble was the bomber had had time to zip far enough from the house that no one would be likely to see him, while he was still watching.

"He'd have been less visible approaching if he'd been driving, especially if he'd had a van. If he was on foot..."

"Either way," Nolan said grimly, "*somebody* had to have seen him."

The medical examiner's vehicle bore the body away. Agent Gordon raised his eyebrows at Nolan. "Don't suppose we'll have any trouble getting reinforcements now."

He grimaced. "No. A few people would be useful. Beyond that, I hope they don't go overboard. This town is too small for a hundred feds to show up."

From expressions, Roanne had the distinct impression they all shared that opinion.

"Let's go see what's happening at the courthouse,"

Nolan said to her. "We'll find the bomber when we figure out how he got that package onto the judge's desk."

She agreed. That had been a lot trickier than setting a package on a welcome mat in a neighborhood where yards were big and shrubs mature.

NOLAN HADN'T BEEN kidding when he'd told Roanne a second bomb would bring federal agents swarming Rosendaal. Four or five more, he could have used. Did use, in fact; he set the first couple of agents from the Seattle office to interviewing everyone who worked in the prosecutor's wing of the courthouse. Their efforts generated yet more names, from a wife who'd brought her husband lunch so he could work steadily throughout the day to defense attorneys aplenty. Parents of children in trouble with the law had been around, as had some teenagers displaying violent tendencies. The guardian ad litem program was housed in the wing.

Another agent grilled security employees again. Yet another took over the canvassing Nolan and Roanne had begun that morning.

Most names gathered were people who could be eliminated because, once again, their window of opportunity was limited. The judge was sure the package hadn't been on his desk when he'd eaten lunch in his office. He recalled a scant pile of mail, which had grown by the end of the day when he started opening it. *Somebody* had inserted the damn thing between around one o'clock and four forty when he'd returned to his office.

Nolan and Roanne hunted down the maintenance workers who had repaired a leaking pipe and entered the courtroom to be sure they didn't miss anything. The first had been employed by the company for at least ten years.

Roanne had looked startled the minute he appeared. "Mr. Zabrowski! I haven't seen you in ages. Stephanie, either."

The graying man smiled and lowered himself to a chair. "Steph is married. Believe it or not, to a national park ranger. He just got transferred to Shenandoah in Virginia. So far, Steph's liking it. She was able to pick up a job teaching kindergarten."

"That's great. You tell her hi from me."

He beamed at her. "Will do." Then he looked from Roanne to Nolan. "This about that damned bomb?"

"Yes. The first of two, if you hadn't heard."

He hadn't and was shaking his head once she told him about the morning's events. "What kind of sick person does something like that?"

Nolan sat back and let her run with this interview, given her comfort with the maintenance man.

"That's what we're trying to find out," she said, voice warm enough to sound as if she were talking to a friend. "You were in the courthouse the day the bomb was planted on Judge Anderson's desk. Can you tell me what time of day you were there, and for how long?"

"Didn't take us fifteen minutes to confirm there were no leaks there. Guess it must have been..." His forehead crinkled in thought. "Almost lunch time. Noonish?"

"Did you see anyone else at all while you were there, besides the guard at the door?"

"Well, I was working with a new young guy. Had been all week. He seems to know what he's doing."

Raul Lopez, it seemed, had grown up in California but moved to Washington following a young woman. The move had occurred three or four years ago. He was engaged to Ana Hernandez, who waitressed at a café Nolan had noticed in passing.

"You didn't see anyone else?" Roanne asked.

"Not a soul."

She smiled at him. "Okay. If Mr. Lopez is here, will you send him in?"

"You betcha."

Zabrowski heaved himself to his feet and ambled out. Nolan used the time to look up Raul Lopez and his Ana.

"Lopez got into some legal trouble when he first moved here," he told Roanne, eyes on his laptop screen. "Bar fight, manslaughter. And guess who he appeared before?"

"Judge Anderson. That's a serious charge. Why isn't he in prison?"

Nolan grunted. "A witness spoke up and named another man. Police didn't find a knife on Raul, although he could have gotten rid of it."

"The time frame is right."

"It is. But why would he be so angry when he got off?"

"Because he lost the girlfriend he'd followed to Rosendaal?"

Still scanning the information he'd pulled up, Nolan said, "Guess who one of the investigators was? And…his case was assigned to Whitley."

"You're saying it was my investigation?" Roanne's forehead wrinkled. "I don't remember that one."

A knock on the door interrupted their speculation.

A handsome man strode in, wearing the company's navy blue uniform with a name tag. His gaze locked on Roanne. "I remember you."

"You look only vaguely familiar. I'm sorry. I'm Detective Roanne Engle, and this is FBI agent Nolan Cantrell."

Nolan waved the man to the seat facing the table behind where he and Roanne sat.

Raul spoke up again. "You're not the one who arrested me. I didn't know anyone was even looking at the possibility I hadn't stabbed that guy. I thought I was the easy answer and nobody would consider digging deeper. You're the one who found a witness who saw what really happened."

Her face cleared. "Oh, I do remember that. I'm not sure I ever met you."

"I saw you a few times." He hesitated. "I should have found you to say thanks."

"I was just doing my job." She smiled. "Your record is clean since."

His short laugh didn't hold much humor. "My girlfriend gave me hell. If I have a beer now, it's at home."

"Good for you."

"Did the arrest make you mad?" Nolan asked.

He gave Nolan an incredulous glance. "I wasn't even *with* the two men who started the fight. Everything just got crazy. You know?"

"It must have been scary."

His shoulders moved. "Zabrowski said you're investigating who may have set that bomb."

"We are. Two bombs now."

"What?"

Nolan took a turn describing that morning's horror. "Because today's victim was the prosecutor assigned to you and your appearance was in front of Judge Anderson, you can see why we needed to talk to you."

Lopez lurched to his feet, knocking his chair back. "You think *I'd* do something like that?"

Nolan's gut said no, although once they learned more

about Lopez, they could revisit the possibility of him being a suspect.

"At this point, we're talking to everyone who was in the courthouse that day. The guard at the door mentioned you and your partner. I gather that it was mid-morning when you checked for leaks."

"Yes!"

"You didn't return to do any follow up that day."

He yanked his chair forward and sat down again. "No. Why would we? We spent the afternoon plumbing a house out at that new development, Tulip Fields."

Out of the corner of his eye, Nolan saw Roanne wrinkle her nose and grinned. Builders and city officials did go overboard with the tulip references.

She nailed Lopez down on times, then talked about this morning. If he were being honest, he'd been finishing breakfast with his girlfriend. "Ask her!"

"We may do that," Nolan said. "As I said, what I'm most interested in was whether you saw anyone at the courthouse that morning."

"Not that I remember. There was a guard at the door." He scratched his jaw. "Otherwise, the basement seemed to be mostly storage, pipes, furnace. You know, that kind of thing."

They finally let him go, neither saying a word until the door swung shut behind him.

"I don't see it," Roanne said.

Nolan stretched his arms over his head, hearing a few creaks. Seeing amusement on Roanne's face, he grimaced. "Come on, you must have a few aches and pains, too. It hasn't been that long since you were almost blown up."

"Nice way to put it. Yes, I do. Then there's the bruises." She touched one cheek. "You know it was broken."

He studied her more carefully. "You've covered the discoloration."

She had an exceptionally mobile face. "If you look closely, you can see the bruises."

"I can, but you did a good job." His voice was huskier than it should have been. The awareness of the damage she'd sustained, of how easily she could have been killed, awakened a sharp pain beneath his sternum. Actually, the reminder was probably a timely one. He wanted her. Acting on the desire would violate the rules he lived by. Hurting her would be even worse.

Focus on your job, he ordered himself. Frowning, he said, "What next?"

CHILLED BY NOLAN's obvious withdrawal, Roanne strove for professionalism, hoping she hadn't blushed at what she'd imagined she saw in his gaze.

"Talk to the office-equipment guy. He works for a local company called Quick Response, Get It Done Right. I've left a couple of messages, but he hasn't responded."

"Let's just show up."

"Why not?"

The drive was half a dozen blocks, if that. Neither spoke. Quick Response was on the outskirts of the city's modest downtown, housed in a nondescript stucco building.

They entered to find a pleasant-faced older woman sitting behind a desk and a computer monitor. Her eyes widened at the sight of their badges.

"Can I help you?"

"Yes, we'd like to speak to Blaine Weightman."

"Oh, I'm sorry! He's out on a job." Looking anxious,

she said, "Can Mr. Weightman's employee help you? I think I heard him coming in the back."

"I'm afraid not. This has to do with the bombing at the courthouse. Can you tell us where to find him? Or call and ask if we can get together?"

"Well... I'll try calling." As she dialed, a young guy emerged from the back and hovered in the doorway, listening.

Clearly, Weightman did answer the phone. The secretary covered the speaker to convey his request that the cops stop by the office an hour or an hour and a half from now.

More than a little irritated, Roanne agreed. She then asked to look at the schedule for the past week. Weightman had been at the courthouse and one of the wings for close to two hours on the day in question.

"Do you work with someone else?" she asked the young guy.

"You mean to fix things? Hardly ever," he said. "Most office machines are relatively compact. There's no need and no room for a second person."

She thanked him, nodded at the office manager and led her and Nolan's departure.

Chapter Nine

Three unmarked official vehicles with a forest of antennae half-filled the small parking lot in front of the café.

"Is this part of the swarm?" Roanne asked politely, a dimple betraying her amusement.

Nolan huffed. "Undoubtedly. We'll be stumbling over them before you know it."

"Do you want to try somewhere different?"

"Can we get food to go and sit in the park?"

"That sounds good." She directed him to a taco stand she liked.

Once he handed her the bags of food, she heard his stomach rumble at the smell. He steered them toward the river park, where at this time of day there were plenty of empty tables.

Swinging a leg over the bench, she said, "Now that you have so many minions, you won't need me."

"No." His blue eyes had never looked so bright—and so penetrating. "You're the only member of this team who knows the terrain, so to speak. Plus—"

He stopped so fast, she heard the skid.

"Plus?"

"You won't like this, but I'd worry about you." His jaw muscles flexed. "I already worry about you at night."

Her eyes narrowed. "Because I'm a woman."

"Because you're a target. We know that."

The reminder stirred disquiet she didn't want to acknowledge. "He could have planted a bomb in my garbage, but he didn't," she pointed out.

He grunted and took a bite. Oh, she wanted to quarrel with him. Surely they could cover more ground if they split up—but she liked working with him. Her hair-raising experience with the courthouse bomb had left her with anxiety she didn't want to acknowledge.

So all she said was "We have an hour. What do you want to do with it?"

"Take a look at the cult grounds."

Surprised, Roanne said, "It's not that exciting. And we've confirmed that their guru is still behind bars."

"But there were—or are—other cult members. Maybe one has been simmering all this time."

"Seems like it's been too long."

"The cult is the one thing that stands out in this town."

"Except the tulips."

One corner of his mouth turned up. "Hard to miss 'em. I might enjoy seeing the fields if I wasn't here to work."

"You're right."

Once they'd finished their lunch, he stood with apparent reluctance, stretched his arms over his head and tossed the food bag into a trash can. When Roanne saw his expression change, she was more aware of the guardedness than usual.

Neither said a word until they'd gotten into his SUV—her home away from home these days—and backed out. She offered directions to a place that had given her the creeps ever since they learned even part of what had happened there.

The drive took them south along the river. At first sight, the entry to Theodoros's territory was no different than to other neighborhoods here on the flood lands between Rosendaal and the next town, except the gravel road wasn't being maintained. A front wheel lurched into a cavernous hole, and Nolan gritted his teeth.

Roanne made a face. "Back when I was interviewing cult members, I'm sure the whole neighborhood, and especially the road, wasn't so rundown."

"I guess the great leader forgot to leave instructions for his followers."

She wrinkled her nose, drawing Nolan's attention. "I doubt the great leader gave a damn about anyone but himself."

"No wife? Kids?"

"I doubt he ever had any interest in a long-term relationship with a woman. And what woman would put up with a husband who samples other women on a regular basis? Just imagine, any of the women in the cult who got pregnant had to wonder if the baby was their husband's or Fedor's."

"Can't imagine a woman worshipping a man to that extent, either." Roanne couldn't help seeing his fingers tighten on the steering wheel until his knuckles were white. Nolan, she suspected, would be possessive if he ever did fall in love. "Being in the husband's position wouldn't sit well with most men."

"There may have been people who moved here and were initially, er, impassioned by Fedor. Even in court, he projected a burning kind of dominance that made me shiver." She wrinkled her nose, then glanced at him. She had to laugh at his expression. "No, not that kind of shivering.

"Anyway—" she shrugged "—back to our current focus. Why would an angry husband have a grudge against the court system that convicted and sent good ol' Fedor to prison?"

"You're right, but the existence of the cult nags at me. This seems to be a peaceful town. Your friendly neighborhood cult is an anomaly."

"A lot of people in town thought it was a blight," she admitted. "As I said, some people from the cult held jobs in town. Overall, townspeople tried really hard to pretend Fedor and company weren't here."

As they zigzagged to avoid the molar-breaking potholes, she couldn't help noticing how dry the thin forest here was. If the hemlock and fir and cedar started dying, that wouldn't be the biggest worry for most parts hereabout. Nope, tulips and to a lesser degree, other bulbs, were the economic driver for Rosendaal and Mount Vernon.

They emerged into a large clearing surrounded by probably thirty small log cabins and run-down mobile homes. The largest looked like a lodge in a national park and was in a lot better shape than the other buildings. Out of fear or faith that their intrepid leader would soon be released from the correctional institute?

A few of the shabby homes were surrounded by flowers, fewer had porches. Fruit trees were plentiful, making her assume the cult members strove for self-sufficiency. A stretch of land ahead was being farmed. The corn was easy for her to identify, and she thought she recognized peas, but one green field looked an awful like another. These folks weren't bothering with tulips, at least.

Some of the homes were deteriorating and vacant. The few people outside on porches or wielding a hoe in the nearest fields stopped what they were doing, straightened and stared at the strangers.

Roanne spotted a couple of boys who might've been seven or eight. One wore denim overalls with no shirt beneath, which revealed sunburned shoulders, blistered skin and bones. The other boy's oversize T-shirt could have been his father's. The hem hit him at mid-thigh. Shorts were barely visible below the hem. Both boys were barefoot and dirty.

Nolan swore under his breath. "I've seen more livable villages in impoverished parts of the world after a bomb blast."

"I need to alert social services," she said in dismay. "I doubt those kids are in school. Any teacher would have called Child Protective Services."

"We can hope so," he said, his eyes on the mirror.

"They have to be brothers." Roanne looked over her shoulder to keep the boys in sight.

"Real close together in age." They glanced at each other, sharing the same thought.

He drove the circle slowly. Every house seemed more dilapidated than the last. What few people she'd seen earlier had retreated inside or stepped just out of sight. She was startled when a man, radiating hostility, stepped out on the road when they were two-thirds of the way around the circle.

Nolan's hand lowered to the hilt of his gun, even though the guy didn't appear to have a weapon. *Appear* wasn't a meaningful word to any cop. The man's hands were fisted at his side and his face was twisted with anger. Nolan swerved so that his right tires rested on brown grass to the side of the road. He braked right beside the one person who appeared to want to talk to them, rolled down the driver's-side window, then nodded civilly. Roanne admired his calm.

The man demanded, "Who are you, and what do you want?"

Nolan's fingers flexed. Roanne stiffened and let her hand drift toward the weapon she wore on her hip. If this guy made one wrong move...

Nolan spoke calmly, however, as if surprised to be questioned. "Is this a private road? I apologize if so. I'm FBI Special Agent Nolan Cantrell. I was curious, and Detective Engle gave me directions." He nodded to the side. "Looks like the fields could use a good rainfall."

Gray streaked brown hair, and the face was heavily lined. Not from age, she suspected, but because of poor nutrition and anger. After a moment, he said gruffly, "We're folks trying to get by. That's all. What's the FBI want with us?"

"Right now, nothing." Nolan kept his tone easy. "I'm in town because of the bomb at the courthouse. You must have heard about it."

"Are we condemned because we once belonged to a commune?"

"Once? Looks like a lot of you stayed on."

"You know how high rent is these days? I'd like a big house with a view, like that judge owns," he said acidly. "Or—" his gaze narrowed on Roanne "—like that real pretty house Detective Engle owns. Nice garden. Bet she's on city water, instead of trying to suck up what we can from a failing well."

Her nerves twitched. How did he know where she lived? How often had he driven by her house?

She leaned forward and said, "The county has a program to help finance new wells. If you'll give me your name—"

His laugh was one of the darkest sounds she had ever heard. "I remember you. I don't trust you."

Her face hardened. "Fedor beat a child to death. He raped a lot of women."

"Wasn't rape," the man mumbled.

"Close enough," Roanne said crisply. "You're defending Theodoros after he hurt all those children? Did he summon any of *your* kids to be 'disciplined'?"

His mouth tightened. His Adam's apple bobbed. "No," he said finally.

More quietly, Roanne said, "I acted on behalf of the children."

"Don't mean you're welcome here."

Nolan's shoulders tightened. "Where were you Monday morning? Can you *prove* you weren't near the courthouse?"

The guy shuffled back. "I had nothing to do with that! Why are you questioning *me*?"

"People who haven't committed a crime, and don't plan to, are likely to be pleasant when a police officer rolls down the car window to chat. You came out firing—"

"What are you talking about? I don't got a gun!"

"I'll bet you have one in your house."

Or tucked at the back of his waistband. If so, he didn't make a move for it. He just continued glaring at Nolan, who kept his expression hard.

Grudgingly, the cultist said, "Got a hunting rifle, sure. But you were asking about a bomb, not a shooting. I was in Iraq and don't want nothing to do with bombs ever again."

She'd swear Nolan's shoulders eased. These two were compatriots of a sort, understanding each other's history.

"I feel the same," he said, the tone of voice dialed back. "That's why I want to get my hands on a bomb maker who doesn't mind young children being collateral damage."

"What are you talking about? What I heard was it was a bomb that went off at the courthouse. Seems kind of stupid to me when if you hate someone's guts, you could just shoot 'em. Over there, a lot of people killed themselves by accident with their own bombs."

"Yes." Nolan held his gaze. "I was there, too. I defused bombs."

For a moment, they kept staring at each other. Then Nolan nodded, released the emergency brake and started forward.

The man, bitterness still visible, stayed on the road, watching them go.

NOLAN KEPT HIS eye on his rearview mirror until they'd reached the highway. Then he shook his head. "I don't like him knowing where you and the judge both live. Why would he have taken the trouble to find out? He may have driven by your place and saw you gardening or pulling into the driveway. But Judge Anderson? His home isn't on the way to anyplace else."

"No." Perturbed, she didn't say anything else.

Nolan watched her out of the corner of his eye for a minute before saying, "You have a headache."

"I do, but I'll survive."

"Let's stop for a cold drink somewhere and a chance for you to take a painkiller."

Roanne didn't attempt any defensiveness. Her voice was quieter than he liked, though. "I did take some Tylenol earlier."

"The doctor gave you something stronger than that."

"Yeah, but it makes me feel muddled. I'd rather wait until I get home. Anyway, we don't want to miss talking to Blaine Weightman."

His gaze arrowed on the drive-through connected to a local deli. Without consulting her further, he put on his signal and turned into it.

"Hey!"

"This isn't negotiable."

She growled at him but handed over a five-dollar bill and asked for a lemonade. By the time he gave it to her, she had shaken a pill into her palm.

He bought a cola and drank thirstily. "Was that so bad?"

Roanne sighed. "No. I'm just opposed to taking orders. Do too much of that, I look weak."

Nolan snorted. "Weak people don't toss a bomb as if they're a major league pitcher, then somehow vault ten feet or more to escape the blast zone."

She made a face at him. "Oh, fine."

Nolan laughed, the dent in his cheek looking good. He barely glancing down at his phone, which had been buzzing all day.

"Are you going to ignore all the texts, not to mention some calls?"

"If I can get away with it. I'm supposed to be supervising a major investigation, but I seem to have also been designated as the housing director. Nobody is happy to find the town so overcrowded. Tourists and the rooms the ATF agents nabbed early on mean newcomers are lucky if they can get a place to lay down their head out at a freeway hotel."

"Like I said, Dad has two guest rooms. I'm sure he'd

be glad to put up a couple of agents. That doesn't offer a lot of privacy—" She hesitated.

"If I were you," he said cautiously, "I'd worry about your father overhearing too much. He's already scared."

"You're right."

Nolan was pleased to have eased the conversation in the direction he'd hoped for. "Do you have a spare room?"

Was she blushing? "No. Sorry."

He shifted focus. "We're here, and there's a parking place. Just give it some thought. In the meantime, I don't like Weightman dodging us."

"Maybe he had an urgent job? Small businessmen and women can't afford to be a no-show."

"You think of an excuse to let anyone off the hook."

She huffed. "An interview goes better if neither of you are already bristling."

"Cops can't afford to be too sympathetic."

She made a sound that might be "Pshaw" before adding, "Did you miss the second parking slot?" These days, those were in short supply, too. Her disappointment at the sight of a pickup pulling out of a spot halfway down the block amused him.

He couldn't let himself laugh, though. What's more, he should have kept his mouth shut, Nolan realized, if he wanted an invite into her house. Which he did, for multiple reasons: It would help with the no-vacancy problem—and he was willing to bet she had at least a sofa bed. Near enough to hear her soft sighs or tiny cries felt right. Being so close to her during the night reminded him of that first night, when he'd been so grateful to have her readily reach for him.

When he'd first thought *Uh-oh* because he'd held her hand, sensed her distress as if they had clicked. Not a vision he'd prepared for.

BACKING INTO the open place at the curb, Nolan stole a glance at Roanne. Stress was visible on her face, and her hair had escaped the bun at her nape to curl around her temples and forehead. He could tell from some giveaway lines that the painkiller hadn't kicked in yet. No, he especially didn't like the idea of her being alone when she wasn't at her sharpest.

Of course, she'd be annoyed if he told her that. She'd ask if he fussed over men he worked with when they didn't look best.

The answer was no.

They sat quietly where they were, finishing their drinks.

"Dad would be thrilled with you as a roommate."

He grinned. "See? You're a softy."

She scowled even as her eyes twinkled, and said, "I must be. Poor Dad."

Still smiling, he opened his door when there was a break in traffic. She followed suit.

"Weightman had better be here," he grumbled.

"The guy services copy machines."

Nolan waited for her to join him on the street. "Which requires the skill set we're looking for."

Her mouth opened and closed.

"And he had an excuse to be at the courthouse—and just about anywhere else he wants to be." He started across the street, then realized she hadn't joined him.

Just as he turned back, she shook her head and hurried to catch up.

He gripped her upper arm. "What was that about?"

Looking perturbed, she said, "Just...thinking you're right. This is a guy who knows what wire goes where to spark a reaction. And...everyone else we've talked to today has made himself readily available."

"Do you know him?"

Their reflections showed in the plate-glass windows that faced the street. Nolan wasn't the only one studying her.

"I'm not sure. I've seen workmen at the police department hunched over printers and copiers and who knows what. I've never had reason to pay attention."

Which might not mean a thing. Nolan knew he didn't snap to attention just because he idly noticed someone working on an office machine, either, so long as they weren't within earshot. But in this case... Roanne was more observant about people she saw in passing than he was. He was bothered by her expression, both thoughtful and a little uneasy.

Chapter Ten

The minute the receptionist showed them into Blaine Weightman's office, Roanne vaguely recognized him. She'd probably nod if they passed in the grocery store. He was younger than she'd recalled, maybe in his late twenties. Good-looking guy with blond hair and gray eyes. There was some reason he'd caught her attention. Maybe because he'd eyed her in a way that had discomfited her?

He rose from behind his desk and smiled. "Detective Engle. You called me in that time when a low-life wearing butt-kicking boots battered the copier at the station within an inch of its life."

She lifted her eyebrows. "Within an inch of its life? I seem to remember we buried the thing. Chief wasn't happy."

He laughed heartily. "Yeah, there was no hope of putting the pieces together again. But you know, Chief Breck never is happy."

Even as she chuckled, she didn't miss the barb he'd tossed out. "He's happy when he's in front of the cameras after we make a big arrest," she conceded. "Speaking of—"

"Don't tell me. This about the bombing?"

"Meet Special Agent Cantrell. He's leading the FBI response to the bombing."

Weightman's mobile face immediately sobered. He came forward and shook Nolan's hand. "You couldn't have anyone better to back you up, Agent Cantrell."

Why would he say that, as little contact as they'd had?

Nolan only said blandly, "So I'm finding."

Weightman mentioned he'd been called that morning for a couple of jobs as well as the one that had kept them waiting. He'd barely sat down when his phone range. He wheeled his chair away to keep his voice low and spoke brusquely. The moment that call ended, he pulled a facade of good humor over his face again.

"I suppose you want to know why I was at the courtroom the day of the bombing. A shocker, wasn't it? I was long gone before your heroics, thank God, because the blast and screams traumatized the folks who were still there, or so I hear. Reason I'd been there in the first place was the copier that judges and their assistants use had glitches. So yes, I was upstairs in the wing from one until... I don't know. After splitting up, Jeff and I got a couple of smaller jobs done, too."

In other words, he'd put himself in place and in the right time to have slid the bomb into Judge's Anderson's pile of mail. Was he naive enough not to guess what triggered their questions?

Which jobs had demanded only one of them?

Nolan sat back and let her take charge. She nailed Weightman down on what else they'd been needed to fix and who had handled each job. He watched closely as she made notes.

"Early on, we carried in and set up a decent-quality laminate desk to replace the original, cheap one at a rookie cop's desk. That's easier as a two-person job. Once the pieces were there, I was able to get back to that dinosaur of a copier. Don't think it's got much life in it, either."

Was she imagining a smirk?

"Did you bring the desk and your tools in through the back door?" Nolan asked.

"We almost always do. Not to complain, but dirty, uniformed maintenance folks hauling equipment don't enhance the solemnity of our halls of justice. We're necessary but the kind of people you hustle out the back when your guests are coming in the front."

She didn't believe his rueful smile.

His gaze arrowed in on Roanne. With a shrug, he said, "I bet you didn't really remember me, for example. Attitudes like that get to you sometimes. Tell you the truth, when I bought the business last fall, I didn't think through how fast technology is making us obsolete. I should have wondered why it was being sold for a song. Printers, copiers make up most of our repairs. We're trying to compete with Office Depot and similar businesses by delivering our products within the county and assembling them, too. We're faster than any competitor for the right paper, envelopes, whatever. Repair has almost become a sidelight. Now we're an office-supply store, doing what we have to, mostly undercutting prices of my major competitors. So far, so good, but we can never let up."

Why the speech? Did Weightman need to feel as if he was a big businessman, patient enough to answer questions as long as he could circle around them? Roanne was left with a tinge of embarrassment, given that he was right: She *hadn't* recognized him initially, and when she did, that memory was filed in her *clerks, gas-station atten-*

dants and the drivers that flung packages at their recipients before running back to the trucks category.

What better distraction than to needle her?

Nolan stirred. Did he not like Weightman's focus on her? "Since you say the copiers hardly ever work right, I'd expect you to keep busy with that alone for now."

"Well. Copiers aren't used as heavily as they used to be, not with the shift to digital." He shifted in his chair. "I shouldn't prattle. You must have more questions for me."

"We do," Nolan agreed. "Especially now that we know you were *in* the courthouse, not just in the basement and the wing where the prosecutors have their offices."

New discomfort flickered across Weightman's face before he appeared puzzled. "The courthouse and police department are among my biggest customers. What can I tell you?"

Was he really not getting it, or did he wander in and out so often and chat with staff that it never occurred to him that investigators could suspect him?

"We're collecting names," she said. "Did you see anyone that day who surprised you, if only because it wasn't a place you'd expect to see them?"

"I saw Bob Farrant," he blurted. With an awkward shrug, he said, "I guess I thought—"

Roanne jotted down the name. She'd ticketed Farrant once herself.

"Heard some thumps coming from Judge MacGregor's office then voices. One of them was a woman. I didn't wait to come face-to-face with her, but I guess it's no secret."

Roanne didn't bother pointing out that a good percent of the prosecuting or defense attorneys, never mind clerks, bailiffs, research assistants and others, were women. A man and woman's voices behind a closed door did not count as a scandal. Yes, she'd already heard that a married judge was involved with a woman, and even who that woman was. Unless she was investigating a crime, personal relationships were none of her business.

She and Nolan ended up with half a page long list of names, although she wondered about the accuracy of the information. Was Blaine sure he'd seen such-and-so on Monday and not the previous Friday? Well, no, but… Had he happened to glance into Judge Anderson's office? Maybe noticed a pile of mail on his desk?

"Can't think why I would have. I go by his office two or three times a week. Anytime I'm at the courthouse, I walk past a couple of dozen offices. They just don't register."

"Was your assistant upstairs at all with you when you were in the courthouse itself?" Nolan asked. His tone was more casual than his cold eyes.

Blaine rocked back. "Ah…can't say. Probably not. We work faster alone. I heard his voice. Seems like he might have flirted with a girl he wants to start something with. She's an assistant to Judge Foster, down the end of the hall."

"Would your front desk employee be able to nail down your precise schedule better than you can?"

If Blaine had imagined the two law enforcement officers had visited to take advantage of his insider knowledge of the court house, he must've been getting a little nervous.

"She schedules our jobs in a broad sense, but if something urgent comes up, she calls our mobile phones."

"Do you have cards with those numbers?" Nolan inquired.

Blaine produced two of them, his gaze a lot warier than it had been.

Roanne thanked him, Nolan nodded curtly and they walked out. A few furrows deepened existing lines on his forehead as they departed the office store and crossed the street to his vehicle.

She got in first, then saw that he was talking on his phone and pacing. She'd noticed his leashed energy before and wondered if his parents had had to pin him down to make him get his homework done.

Although maybe not; he was also a driven man, which probably meant he took every assignment seriously.

When he ended the call, she asked, "Anything I should know?"

"Later."

In other words, not having to do with a suspect.

"What do you think about Weightman?"

Nolan's face tightened. "He's slick. I don't like it. What little he shared was salacious."

Roanne made a face. "He likes to be in the know but not seen as a gossip."

"He wanted to impress you," Nolan said dryly.

"I didn't get that." That wasn't quite true but was definitely irrelevant.

"He'd have been real glad if I'd had a call and left you alone with him. His whole attention was on you."

"Is that why you looked so stony? Because he was fixated on me?"

"Partly."

She debated calling Nolan on imagining that he had any say in her social life but decided quarreling when they were out in public wasn't good for careers. Especially since she had zero interest in Blaine. Instead, she asked, "What's the other part?"

"I think he was playing us, and I don't like it."

"That crossed my mind."

"He couldn't imagine why we were asking *him* about his whereabouts. Thus the other suspects."

"Blaine's easygoing schtick must work for a salesman."

"Question is was he genuinely comfortable answering questions and it never occurred to him they were really aimed at him, or was this his cover?"

"Good-looking guy," she said. "Is he married? Does he have family? How long has he lived here? I keep thinking—"

Agent Cantrell had one of the sexiest smiles she'd ever seen but right now he was annoyed. What had she said? It surely wasn't her comment about Blaine's handsome features. Why would that bother him?

She ducked to peer at herself in the passenger mirror, winced and dismissed any possibility a man who looked like him could have a thing for her, even if a few times she'd imagined seeing a glint in his eyes. At her best, she didn't have many men coming on to her. Female cops were a turn-off for many men. The cover-up she'd applied to hide the remnants of her bruises that morning had worn off, and tiny hairs had pulled lose from her usually neat ponytail or bun. Her freckles emphasized the pallidness of her skin.

She sighed and turned her mind to her job just as Nolan spoke.

"Why would Weightman buy a dying business? Was he fooled? We can go back and verify his calls out with his secretary."

Roanne blinked. Great idea, except the woman hadn't been present when they left. And what about the young partner or assistant. Had they even gotten his name? Could be he was more observant than his boss. In fact, how much of the day *had* the two spent together? Most of it? None of it? She mentioned him and said, "We know he was at the courthouse and has the same skill set as Blaine. We shouldn't have dismissed him."

"Do you know Weightman better than you implied?" Faint irritation curled Nolan's mouth.

"Do you have a problem with him other than that he was unwilling to even speculate on what times he happened to be wandering in what part of the courthouse?"

Nathan said curtly, "He rubbed me the wrong way."

"Are we talking about personality? Likelihood he's a mad bomber? Or are you just frustrated because we keep coming up with dead ends?"

He frowned. "I wouldn't say we are. Weightman ticks off too many boxes."

She couldn't argue. "A lot of anger there."

"Good with putting small electronics together."

"Happens to have been in the right place at the wrong moment—or vice versus."

"You're right. We've been skating the surface too often. Does he have family? Belong to a bowling league? What does he do with his spare time? Did he already live in Rosendaal when he bought the business, or did he move here from somewhere else? What about past jobs?"

"Have he and Curtis Whitley had any prior contact?" she contributed.

"Not to mention where was he this morning?"

Roanne pondered the exchange. It was a little deflating to confirm that Nolan's prickliness had nothing to do with how Blaine had or hadn't looked at her.

"I feel incompetent," she announced.

Nolan flashed a smile. "Me, too. Although, in fairness, this was supposed to be yet another conversation that would allow us to rule him out, as we have half the townspeople we've talked to."

"Why don't we deploy your FBI troops to have more of these conversations?"

"I want someone to talk to every person who has an office on that floor and possibly expand it to the entire building. Assistants included. In fact, we should have expanded those interviews sooner."

"The trouble is there are too many people in and out of the building. And with this being a small town, they all know each other."

"Whitley and the judge are sure to have been in the same courtroom more than a few times."

"But Weightman?"

"If Whitley had been a defense attorney, the connection between them might give us somewhere to look. As it is…" Nolan scowled. "The sunny citizens of Rosendaal shouldn't be so damn trusting."

She wrinkled her nose. "Trust me, plenty of them are guilty of domestic abuse, drug abuse and general ugly behavior. Given my job, I know." She sighed. "Whoever our perpetrator turns out to be, I've had a lesson in what happens when security on a public institution is inadequate. Since I moved back to town, I've hammered everyone with the need for better security. What I didn't realize is that front-door and back-door electronic surveillance still wouldn't be enough. We should have guards wandering the halls, inquiring what visitors' purpose is in that building, why they'd just come out of a particular office or storage room. Ask to see the contents of packages—and they need to be on their toes even with the sunny people they know."

He was kind enough to keep his mouth shut.

"I have a question," she said.

"Yes?"

"Why are we ignoring the latest bomb blast? Have you assigned other agents to that?"

"I have," he said imperturbably. "But I keep coming back to the one you heaved as if it was a javelin."

"I prefer throwing myself over a bar in competitions rather than tossing a dangerous object."

"Good decision." He braked for a red light, his fingers tapping the steering wheel. "In my opinion the first bomb is key because of the placement. What are the odds we'll find that one of Whitley's neighbor saw a car she didn't recognize parked close by on a side street? Oh, and she noted a license plate number, color, bumper sticker. Then she saw someone trotting back to the car, crossing the Whitley's lawn. If we're really lucky, she recognizes the man. If we're not quite that lucky, she can sketch his face."

Roanne pondered that. "I see your point."

"Other agents can spread their attention. I'd rather focus on security at the courthouse and the number of potential witnesses."

"I agree, but you don't have to belabor our inadequacies. I'm betting the FBI has a way bigger budget than we do."

He made a peace sign, then treated her to another of his sexy grins. "Let's just say if no witness comes forward or Sharon fails to produce a crisp fingerprint or some leap of logic, the bomb on the Whitley's porch is a dead end. And pardon the unpleasant pun."

Roanne would love to have a brilliant leap of logic but remained devoid of them. "What next?"

"It's almost time for the afternoon meeting. Maybe

someone else will have an idea or have spoken to a witness or perp who contradicted himself."

"Did I know about this? Are we going to cram everyone in?"

"The topic was covered during the morning meeting. I'm reasonably sure you were there."

She stuck out her tongue out at him, her mood lightening when he laughed.

"Fine."

"After the meeting, the only important question is what we're having for dinner," he said as he parked behind the courthouse.

"We can each decide that for ourself, can't we?"

"Ah... I seem to find myself homeless."

Her head snapped around.

"Or lacking a hotel room, at the least. If I'm not going to sleep in my SUV, I have to hope you'll take pity on me."

Her eyes slitted. "I'm sure my father—"

"His guest rooms are assigned."

"You had this in mind all along."

"It does make sense." He wasn't all that successful at hiding a smile.

"I don't *have* a guest room. I set up an office at home. The best I can offer is a sofa bed, and to be honest, it's not comfortable."

"Sounds like a deal to me." His tone became more serious. "I can trade in my room—where, to date, I've barely stopped to shower and toss in bed—and move in with you. We're spending our days together anyway."

"You don't think this will light up the law enforcement gossip mill?"

"Nah. Why would it? We're stuffing agents in anywhere that has some approximation of a bed. We may have to start setting up tents in the park. This way, you and I can have fruitful conversations while we wait for the coffee to percolate. Think of the time we've been wasting!"

They swung into the courthouse parking lot, and he set the emergency brake, then turned to look directly at her. Nolan's expression was more serious than she would have expected.

"Where I'm staying doesn't have to be a deep, dark secret, but I'd like it not be obvious even to your neighbors or anyone who happens to drive by. You can go home on your own, I'll park a street away and you can let me in. Consider me backup."

"I'll do that. But don't think you can have the bed while I sleep on the sofa, even if you *are* bigger and more important."

She loved his laugh.

Chapter Eleven

Roanne would be stunned if any brilliant leaps of inspiration surfaced at the end-of-day meeting, which had been transferred from the conference room to a rarely used symposium with a stage in front and rows of padded seats leading up to the two side doors.

Nolan scanned the room, then raised his eyebrows at her. "Why didn't we get the comfortable seats and better visuals before?"

"It wasn't offered," she muttered. "Besides...there were only ten or twelve of us at any of those earlier meetings."

"Yeah, yeah." He quickly was surrounded by a sea of men and women wearing black suits, white shirts and ties. She looked around for a spot where she would be able to see well. She managed a couple of steps before a hand thrust from the crowd to latch on to her arm.

She half turned. "What?"

"You're sitting up front with me."

"Why would I do that?"

"You represent the city. You're my partner."

She opened her mouth, then shut it without further argument. Why waste her breath? Giving up, she hunted down the coffee urns and poured two cups, dumping little packets of sugar and creamer in her blazer jacket. The crowd quieted as she climbed the few steps and chose a seat.

Apparently that was a signal. Nolan broke free a minute later and joined her.

"Thanks for the coffee," he murmured. Giving the crowd a chance to settle down, he stayed on his feet but said in a voice that effortlessly carried throughout this larger space, "Most of you know me. In case there are a few who don't, I'm FBI Special Agent Nolan Cantrell, lead on this investigation. Introduce yourself to me when you can.

"Beside me is RPD Detective Roanne Engle, the one who came the closest to the first bomb. She saved the life of a superior court judge and has since been targeted by our bomber. The detective is working closely with us. Respond to orders from Detective Engle as you would from me."

Gulp.

He introduced several of the ATF agents, who seemingly were strangers to many of the other feds. Sharon had prepared a slideshow that started with the aftermaths of the bombs that had detonated, then worked her way into fragments that Roanne wouldn't have been able to identify if she hadn't seen this visual presentation before. Roanne learned that Sharon and her fellow team members also built replicas of each exploded bomb, both to make sure she understood how it worked and also to save to show a jury when or if these crimes came to trial.

She tensed at the sight of Curtis Whitley's porch, his body in the midst—and his young daughter quaking at the side with a firefighter kneeling protectively. She slid a glance to Nolan, to see it as grim as she remembered even when they reached the scene in person.

Once the slideshow was over, Nolan stood again. "As you see, this bomber has no compunctions. If children are killed by his bomb, he probably won't even bother to shrug. He's as cold-blooded as any I've encountered in my career."

He summed up where the investigation had taken them in the past week, why he'd prioritized the first bomb although he would be assigning agents to approach the crimes from different perspectives.

A woman agent asked, "Detective Engle, how do you see the prank bomb? It seems almost…personal. As if he knows you—or wants to think he does."

She couldn't help but feel unnerved by the sixty or so sets of eyes pinned on her. Beside her, Nolan shifted in his chair, his knuckles brushing her arm. The small touch calmed her.

"That's certainly possible," Roanne agreed. "As you've gathered while you were all trying to find a place to shower and sleep—" a few people laughed "—this is a small city. I grew up here, graduated from high school here. I've only been back for a few years, but I do at least distantly recognize most people. That's been the case through our initial interviews. In some instances, the individual we're interviewing thinks he knows me better than I can imagine he actually does. I've encountered a hint of resentment—but I see that sometimes when I'm pursuing an investigation in my job as a detective for the city as well. At this point, we're undecided whether the prank is a jab at me, in a personal sense, or was designed to increase fear city-wide."

Several individuals debated the likelihood one way or the other, until Agent Donahue from the ATF stood. "I believe the taunt was aimed specifically at Detective Engle.

Whether she was originally a target, she singlehandedly prevented the first and perhaps showiest bomb from succeeding in its intent. She has since been frequently described as a heroine. For the bomber, who wanted to start his campaign of terror with a bang, if you'll forgive the pun, the detective reduced what was intended to be a gory, spectacular beginning to a flop."

Others agreed. As close as she sat to Nolan, Roanne was aware of how rigidly he held himself.

He finally stopped general comment. "You'll all be receiving assignments, but don't hesitate to pursue any oddities." He made a few comments about the ladder of command, but also encouraged the sharing of ideas.

At the last, he said, "It appears our victims and would-be victims may be linked through the court system. Those relationships may turn out to be irrelevant, but at this stage I'm included to believe that link is significant. We all suspect this bomber isn't finished—and chances are good that another would-be victim will be telling."

Someone at the back shouted a question about the cult, which Roanne answered, while reminding everyone that the guru was incarcerated at the state correctional institute and would continue to be so for many years to come.

"The cult has dwindled to a poor neighborhood. Half or more of the members moved away. However, the people lingering feel a lot of anger at authorities. In the packet you've been given, you'll see that we haven't been able to discover any relatives of Theodoras, also known as Dwayne Knepper. Agent Cantrell and I will be pursuing this angle but welcome any information you may encounter."

Escaping the auditorium wasn't easy for Nolan and Roanne—everyone wanted to talk, but eventually he guided her away from the last cluster. In contrast to most of the agents, he'd worn cargo pants and a long-sleeve black tee that said *Police* on the back. His badge and handgun were obvious, unlike those carried by many of the agents dressed in the traditional suits. Seeing him in front of such a large group, Roanne had been aware of his unchallenged air of command. His expression hadn't changed until he and she reached the parking lot in back of the courthouse, which was being patrolled twenty-four seven by a guard Roanne didn't recognize.

"One of your people?" she asked.

"Yes. We assigned full shifts. At least we won't have to worry about our vehicles parked here."

"So mine will be safe to drive now?" The passenger-side door beeped to let her climb into his SUV.

Settling behind the wheel, Nolan gave her a sharp glance. "That will depend on where our personal vehicles are parked at night."

"I have a garage."

"I don't like detached garages."

She rolled her eyes.

"If we're going to work together, it makes sense for us to stay together," Nolan said with finality.

Well, he was right—but Roanne hated letting him get away with deciding what her role would be and where he wanted her. Except, of course, she felt fortunate he'd placed so much trust in her. He could decide at any time that he didn't need her input.

With everything that had been going on, Roanne hadn't let herself look ahead far enough to realize how much her world would shrink when the time came for him to leave.

Did she really know him well enough to miss him?

Roanne was quiet during the short drive to her house. Preoccupied? He swept his eyes between each side and his rearview mirror, not getting even a hint that they were being pursued.

Nolan pulled up in front to let her out. After she opened the door and slid out with a wince she tried to hide, she asked, "You haven't changed your mind?"

"About staying with you? No, unless you really do object. I shouldn't have put you on the spot."

Her smile was weak but real. "No, it's okay. I'll listen for you to knock at the kitchen door."

"I have to pick up my suitcase at the motel."

She only nodded and trudged up her porch sets. He stayed where he was long enough to make sure she inspected her front door and windows before unlocking. Call him paranoid, but he didn't like the shadowy dusk or his sense that the more she was touted for saving the judge, the greater the danger to her.

He wanted to get back to her house, but of course, it took him a good ten minutes to speak to the agents who'd taken over his motel room. They didn't appear to be thrilled by their digs, which had him grinning when he left.

His smile twisted when he remembered Roanne assuring him that her sofa bed wasn't comfortable. Undoubtedly, it would be too short for him, too—but with luck he'd catch a glimpse of Roanne slipping out of the bathroom in her pajamas, her richly colored hair tumbling over her shoulders. He'd have to ask what follow-up she had to do with the doctor. He bet she'd be glad to get rid of the stiffened wrap that kept her from bending her wrist.

After he parked almost two blocks away from her

house, he cut through an alley that bordered the backyard with the dandelions and hopped the fence to Roanne's yard.

Was she a quiet sleeper? Maybe she dated regularly, but he doubted it. Would it bother her to know he was sprawled on her sofa so close? Even as he rapped on her back door, Nolan gave himself a mental slap. He was working with her. She almost had to follow his orders. He had no business wishing she'd invite him into her bedroom.

Nolan inhaled when Roanne let him in. "You've been cooking."

The kitchen held a spicy scent he didn't quite recognize. Her cheeks were a little pink, maybe from the glowing red burner on her stove. "It's a black-bean soup I like. I always make enough to freeze some. I enjoy cooking, but not after a long day at work. I did make some biscuits, though."

"That sounds good."

She'd already changed into a stretchy pair of leggings and an oversize sweatshirt, the combination sexier than she probably realized. Her long, slender legs reminded him of her athletic past, and the baggy shirt didn't hide her generous curves. He liked her bare feet, too—so much smaller than his but with long toes.

While she dished up, he shed his sidearm and holster as well as his badge and the black windbreaker.

"Mind if I get a glass of milk?" he asked.

"Nope. Would you pour me one, too? I had too much coffee today."

He didn't mention that his doctor had hinted at the possibility that Nolan had an ulcer due to his stress level and less than ideal diet.

The minute they sat down, conversation became relaxed. It felt as if they were long-time friends, exchanging snippets of stories from their childhoods or college. No surprise— they'd spent a lot of time together this week.

"How come you weren't decked out in the FBI black and white today?" she asked.

"I visited my sister on the east side of the mountains last week. Got a call and came straight here. I could have asked a friend to pack me some more clothes, but I figure I have an excuse for not wearing a tie. I'm actually getting low on clean clothes." He grinned at her. "I assume a washer and dryer come packaged with my new digs."

She made a face. "You're right. After dinner, I'll throw a load in."

"Of course, that may leave me without anything to wear…"

The dimple in one cheek that she rarely showed off appeared. "I'll lend you my robe. Pink is your color."

"Is it *your* color?"

"No, I look horrible in pink. When I was a little girl, I was into all that princess stuff. Satin pink gown, fake tiara, Mom's high heels that I wobbled in. My hair does better with green or even brown."

Nolan voted for green, but he wasn't so sure pink wouldn't look good, too, with glossy auburn hair.

He offered to clean up while she put the scant leftover soup in the refrigerator, then disappeared to grab sheets, pillows and blankets for the pull-out couch. When Nolan followed her to the living room, he took in the mattress that was maybe full-size.

Roanne inspected it, too. "Okay, now I'm feeling a little guilty."

Nolan laughed. "You warned me."

"Yep. You asked for it. Um, I've pulled all the blinds, but we probably want to avoid the chance someone outside could see that there are two of us."

His lighter mood evaporated. "You're right. We haven't been as careful as we could be."

"Well, I don't know about you, but I'm going to call my dad and then go to bed. He...worries."

"I've noticed." Nolan reached out with one arm to hug her, releasing her a lot sooner than he'd like. "At least you know he isn't lonely."

"Do you know who he got stuck with?"

"Not a clue."

"I thought *you* were in charge." Her lips curved.

"I transferred responsibility. When you're running the show, you can do that." He sat on the edge of the mattress, hiding his wince. Maybe for Christmas he'd buy her a luxurious mattress topper to limit the damage the bars could do.

Hovering in the doorway, arms crossed, she asked, "Do you ever call your parents?"

"Not often," he said tightly. "Sometimes if there's reason for them to think something may have happened to me." Like getting blown up. "I talk a little more often with my sister, but her husband resents me, and she and I aren't close. She's four years younger than I am, for one thing." He paused. "Where your dad is concerned, you're lucky."

Her smile didn't totally work, but she tried. "I am. He doesn't like the idea of letting me go. Sometimes I'm not sure coming home was such a good idea, but..."

"He's happy."

Wrinkled nose, noticeable with the freckles. "Except when he had to sit at my hospital bedside."

"Hey! I seem to remember being the one who sat with you."

Nolan dug through his duffel bag and pulled out pajama bottoms to go with his T-shirt, then pushed back the covers and heaped the pillows.

"So you were." Roanne rarely looked shy, but he guessed having a strange man bedding down in her living room did it. Or maybe it was the memory of him holding her hand through that God awful night or smoothing her hair from her high-curving forehead.

She surprised him. "You were a natural. Dad would have fussed. You just...soothed."

Some grit in his voice, Nolan said, "You don't know how much I wanted to climb into that bed with you. We'd have both slept better."

For a moment, they stared at each other. He couldn't look away, but she shuffled backward as if to escape.

"If you hear a thump in the morning, it's my newspaper."

"Okay. Sleep tight."

This smile finally looked natural. "You, too."

And then the hall light went off, and he stretched out, feeling moody. He'd sleep better tonight if he were sharing her bed, too.

ROANNE PROBABLY HEARD every tiny sound because she was so ultra conscious of her housemate. Either Nolan didn't snore or he wasn't sleeping any better than she was. Now and again, the pull-out sofa squeaked and groaned when he rolled over, but there was more familiar traffic noise out on the street, the neighbor's cat had to be responsible for the thud and scraping sound on the small back porch, and she wished...

She flipped over in bed herself and pressed her pillow over her face, just for a moment. If only Nolan hadn't mentioned her hospital stay and his comforting presence at her bedside. Comforting, she thought, and more.

She did a lot of tossing and turning, not sure if she'd have slept better if she had her house to herself or whether she felt safer with Nolan a room away.

When her alarm went off, she whimpered. A male voice cursed from the living room. Roanne figured she was entitled to the first shower, which helped only a little. Coming face-to-face with Nolan outside the bathroom door, she saw his weariness.

She smiled weakly. "Is this a good time for me to say I told you so?"

Nolan grunted, went into the bathroom and shut the door in her face. Roanne remembered to turn on the dryer to shake wrinkles out of his clothes.

Neither had much to say over breakfast, other than to talk about today's agenda. "I want to go back to the cult," he said. "If our friend Theodorus has any family, someone there must know it."

"I wonder what drove him to going into the guru business. Even with his trial and the witnesses who were willing to speak out, I didn't learn much about his background. I mean, it takes some magic to draw people in. Single kids tend to be introverts."

"True. I spoke to the warden yesterday and asked whether Fedor corresponds with anyone or has visitors. He should get back to me today."

"Isn't that information private?"

Nolan looked faintly surprised. "When I ask, people answer." He grinned at her expression. "I'd better get going."

He disappeared to shave, which didn't wipe the tiredness from his face. "I'll pick you up in front in, say, ten minutes."

Why argue? He dumped some clothes into her laundry basket, tucked everything else he owned neatly in the duffel, then passed her on the way to the back door.

An echo of sound came to her. Just a memory from the night, except alarm sent her dashing to plant herself between him and the door, knocking his hand away before he could grasp the doorknob.

He raised his eyebrows.

"I...heard some odd sounds on the back porch last night. Probably a cat or even a raccoon, but... I don't think you should open that door until we have somebody check it out."

Unblinking, he held her gaze as he took out his phone. It only range twice. "Sharon? I need a favor."

What if both front *and* back were rigged?

Surrounded by a crew of experienced feds, she'd feel like a fool if her imagination had taken a wild leap.

Chapter Twelve

Roanne sank onto a kitchen chair. Neither of them said a word. Nolan paced.

Fortunately, the wait was short. Within ten minutes, two shiny rental SUVs pulled up to the curb in front of Roanne's house. She felt certain the smaller figure dressed in a protective suit was Sharon. The other one could be anyone on the ATF team.

"I'm going to feel silly any minute," Roanne muttered.

A frown tugging at his forehead, Nolan studied her with grave blue eyes. "You have good instincts. And if we're trapped in a bomb-rigged house, are we the only ones? I wish the judge would take a trip."

"And who else is at risk?"

His phone rang. He put it on speaker. "Smart call," Sharon said. "Looks like front *and* back are set with wires wrapped around the doorknobs. We'll take a look at the windows and see if there's a way you two can get out without waiting for us to do our thing."

He swore.

"How did you know?" Sharon asked.

Nolan glanced at Roanne again with those piercing eyes. "My roommate has good instincts. I was reaching for the back doorknob when she leaped in front of me."

Roanne raised her voice. "I...heard some thumps and sort of a shuffling sound during the night. I didn't think anything of it—a neighbor cat visits often, and we have some wildlife. But this morning..." She shivered. "It just...clicked."

"Well, these are nasty ones," Sharon said so cheerfully, Roanne realized the woman positively enjoyed defusing bombs. Or maybe it dissecting them that gave her such pleasure.

"I'm the one who nags you about checking doors carefully before opening them. I'd have walked right into it. I'm glad I'm on this side of both doors," Nolan said, tension adding gravel to his voice. "You saved me."

"I was standing right there, too," she pointed out. "And I'm not sure how we could have seen a trip wire or something like that from inside."

"Yeah." He rolled his shoulders. "We'd better settle down in the dining room. That's central, right?"

Sharon obviously heard, because she said, "I think I'm insulted."

Ignoring the ATF agent's confidence, Roanne mumbled, "My house isn't big. What if the whole thing blows up? Wouldn't one bomb set off the other?"

"That would be bad," Nolan conceded. He dropped his phone into a pocket. "Hey. Come here."

He held out his arms, and she all but threw herself into his embrace. Was she shaking? Maybe—but she thought he was, too.

"Thank God we have experts out there who know how to take care of bombs." Nolan's fervency sounded genuine. "I'm just glad it's not my job anymore."

Roanne held on tight, her voice muffled against his broad, solid chest. "That was...a really close call." She was afraid her teeth were actually chattering. What if she'd seen him die, and in what might've been the most horrible way of all?

"You're a smart woman." He pulled out a chair, sat down and tugged her onto his lap. Roanne stole a peek to be sure the blinds were still pulled. Having the assorted federal agents know Nolan was bedding down here was one thing, but cuddling with her? That could be bad... except she wasn't about to pull away from a man who exuded strength and comfort in a way she'd never known.

He rubbed his cheek against her hair, undoubtedly messing it up, but she didn't care. She lifted her face to kiss his jaw. He went entirely still, gaze locking on her face.

"Roanne?"

Was that a question? She answered by pushing herself up to meet his lips. This kiss wasn't gentle; there was nothing like being scared to heighten emotions. Nolan clasped his hand around the nape of her neck and deepened the kiss. She *needed* his touch, his hunger. She wanted to straddle his lap but had just enough self-restraint to stay sitting on his thighs. If they'd truly been alone...

Nolan lifted his head, and she whimpered.

His voice rough, he said, "I should have someone check on the judge."

"Oh, no!"

He made a call. Then he dropped his phone onto the table with a clunk. "Do you think the bomber knew I was here?"

"Versus him making sure he took care of me whichever way I left the house?" She rested her cheek on his shoulder and tried to corral her flurry of thoughts. "If he followed you and saw where you left your vehicle..."

Nolan swore, then made another call, asking for a sweep of his SUV, too. His arms tightened around her. "If I kiss you again," he said roughly, "I'm not going to want to stop."

She swallowed and nodded. Neither said a word for several minutes.

"I doubt he cares about me," he said. "It's you he's after. He's going to be madder than ever after this."

"Coming in!" Sharon called, just giving Roanne time to slide off Nolan's lap and plop onto another chair. The back door swung open and the ATF agent stepped into the kitchen. "You're free to go. We'll be here for quite a while." Her good humor hadn't diminished.

Hidden beneath the tabletop, Roanne clenched her hands together. "Do you think it'll be safe here tonight if I can get the security company to install cameras and I don't know what else?"

"It'd be better if we find a way to vanish," Nolan said.

Sharon nodded. It was weird talking to someone whose face was obscured. "You can't switch out with someone else."

Horrified, Roanne exclaimed, "No! If somebody else died in my place…"

Nolan reached out to give her a quick, hard hug. "No. Of course not. Maybe an interior room at one of the big hotels in Everett. I'd suggest we go to my place—What is it? An hour drive to Seattle? An hour and a half?—except we'd be too slow responding if another bomb goes off. Early mornings offer too many advantages to the bomber."

"Well, you have time to decide what you're going to do," Sharon said. "We'll be here for a while, unless our boy was even busier last night than we know."

"My car?"

"Nobody touched it. Oh, and the judge's house was

clean. Hearing that yours is rigged scared him enough that he's quit being stubborn. He and his wife are packing."

"He isn't planning to stay with one of his sons, is he?"

"No. He didn't say. They're heading for the airport."

"Thank goodness. One less person to worry about."

Nolan ran a hand over his jaw. Despite his recent shave, Roanne heard a faint rasping sound. "If only we knew who else is on his list of targets."

His grimness was contagious. "Only one way to find out."

When the next bomb detonated.

"I'M TEMPTED TO get this house safeguarded today," Roanne said once she and Nolan pulled away from the curb.

Nolan glanced in his side mirror to see the swarm of protective-suited people on her front porch and lawn. He understood her impulse but said, "You're not going to surprise him with alarms or cameras."

Roanne made a grumbly noise that he thought was cute. Not that he'd ever say so.

"We've got to drop out of sight every night," he said. "I'm going to make sure myself that he didn't put a tracker on my SUV that allows him to follow us easily. In the meantime, it's just as well if he knows you're not home. It's too nice a house to see it blown up."

"Fine. Are we going to the courthouse for the morning meeting?"

Nolan grimaced. These meetings were most often a waste of time, in his opinion, but supervising the increasing law enforcement presence meant he had to show.

"Unfortunately. I want to go back to the cult afterward. This time, we'll go door to door. There have to be people left there that were disillusioned by Fedor and are just stuck for economic reasons."

"I'm still not convinced this is all related to the cult," Roanne said, "but it does bother me that we know so little about Fedor's personal history. If this has to do with him, though, why the couple-year gap?"

"That may become clear once we know more about him and his acolytes."

"What scares me is that this guy is accelerating. How long did it take him last night to rig both doors to my house?"

"Sharon can probably take a guess."

Roanne gripped her seat belt, knuckles showing white. "What if there's more than one perpetrator? There could be two or even more."

"That would be unusual, given the profile we're working with, but let's raise the topic in the morning meeting."

She sniffed. "I don't know about you, but I'm going to be really grumpy if somebody hasn't put on the coffee."

Nolan surprised himself by laughing, despite their near miss—and his intense gratitude. He reached out and took her hand in his. He didn't let go until he had to make a turn.

PAUL ESPOSITO, AN AGENT and profiler Nolan had requested, said "I think it's highly unlikely" when Roanne raised the idea of partners in crime. "Bank robbers come in pairs. Arsonists and bombers, I'm tempted to say never. I may have to eat my words one of these days, but I think if this is related to the cult, the gap in time makes it even more unlikely."

Quite a few people shared Nolan's fixation on the cult, but others expressed skepticism. Fedor had been convicted and imprisoned long enough ago to make him an unlikely motivator.

Nolan didn't comment either way.

Roanne said, "If revenge for Fedor is the reason for this bomber to start his reign of terror, what we need to think about is who else he intends to target. So far, he's gone for the judge, the arresting police officer and the prosecutor. What about the defense attorney who failed to get him off? The social workers who removed the children from the compound? How old were those kids? Any who have become an adult in the intervening years and is angry that his great and glorious leader was forced to face justice?"

The momentary silence told her that everyone was thinking.

Nolan's attention stayed on Roanne. "Who reported the child who died at Fedor's hands? Were there earlier reports about how the children were being treated? Were you primary when the first accusations were made?"

"No, not at the beginning. I didn't get involved until the child was killed." *Child.* Why was she reluctant to say *Dodi*? Because then she saw her battered face? "Even then," she continued, "I was paired with another, more experienced detective who has since retired. At the time, he had a grandson in the same class as the girl who was beaten to death. He was angry. I suspect he'd be glad to talk to us."

"Let's track him down." Nolan made a note on his tablet.

"There had been some reports to Child Protective Services over the course of a year or more," Roanne said. "Those probably aren't in the packets we handed out, because the cult connection is still tenuous. I know the workers weren't entirely convinced by the parents' explanation, but the kids all backed up whatever story the parents told. There were enough concerns, a serious investigation should have been launched. I think the trouble is that one social worker gets assigned to look into why a boy has bruises on his shoulders, but she isn't necessarily aware of other reports. The cult had been here for ten years at least, as I believe I've said before. Many of the members held jobs in the community, and enough kids were enrolled in the public school to avoid scrutiny. Preschool children weren't really on our radar. One or more could have died without us ever knowing."

"Who filed reports?" asked an FBI agent whose name Roanne didn't remember.

"I'll have to pull records to be sure I'm not forgetting anyone, but... I believe it was primarily teachers. Unlike with the judge and the prosecuting attorney, how would the bomber know which of them to target? Especially when none of those initial investigations led to any action?"

"Did anyone put pressure on the school to watch the children who may be at risk?" Nolan asked. "Who was the social worker who handled the death inquiry?"

With chagrin, Roanne realized she already should have been asking these questions.

"Her name is Theresa Bishop. She was—may still be—a supervisor in the department. She was unhappy when she put the pieces of reports and rumor together...too late to save that girl."

Nolan assigned two agents to determine whether Ms. Bishop still lived locally. He wanted them to talk to her and encourage her to go into hiding.

When the meeting broke up and groups were assigned different tasks, including canvassing Roanne's neighborhood for anyone who might have glanced out of a window during the night, she remained troubled.

"Did any adults in the commune report abuse of children?" Nolan asked as they reached his massive vehicle.

"We'd have to look at Child Protective Services records, which usually are kept private, to find out. I think we have reason to do that now, although let's face it—we have to remain aware that the serial bomber may have nothing to do with the cult."

Nolan settled behind the wheel but didn't reach for the key in the ignition. "You're right," he said at last, "and focusing too much attention on the cult, if it turns out to be mistaken, will be my fault."

"Have you ever investigated members of a cult before?" she asked.

"No, and that may be my trouble." He gazed straight ahead, lines deepening on his forehead. "It caught my eye as the one anomaly in your town. Why were they here? What in Rosendaal drew them? Surely not the tulips."

"No, I doubt any of them participated in events around the tulip festival," she said wryly.

"Okay," he said. "Back to my fixation, which I want to continue to focus on until we either rule them out or someone else comes up with a strong lead. We have enough investigators looking at other possibilities. So, what about the girl who was killed? Did her parents protest the 'punishment'? Were they enraged afterward?"

"There was no father in the picture." Reading Nolan's expression, she shook her head. "Dodi's mother was an early convert, a single mother bringing her girl with her. Not much education, scraping by financially, she may have seized on Fedor's preaching and offer of a community and even a house or trailer for herself and her daughter. If she were scared enough about how she could support herself and her child, she may have ignored a lot of early warning signals. At trial, she defended Fedor."

Nolan made a disbelieving sound.

"She kept repeating that Dodi knew one of the few things Fedor asked of them was obedience. It appeared he was grooming her for a sexual conquest, and Dodi knew that was scary or wrong. I remember her mother sobbing on the stand, saying if Dodi had just done what she'd been told, this never would have happened."

The memory still sickened Roanne. Not just the poor girl's brutal death, but the parent who'd chosen to sacrifice her child for what she perceived as security.

"So, she didn't storm into the police station the next day, insisting that creep had beaten her daughter to death."

"No. She even tried to convince us that Dodi was visiting family, that nothing bad had happened to her."

"Unbelievable." Nolan thrust his fingers into his hair and yanked hard. "I don't suppose the woman still lives here."

"I have no idea. Should we find out?"

"Yes." He accelerated fast enough out of the parking lot that she grabbed the strap above her door.

He glanced at her and slowed down. "Sorry. Not much shocks me anymore, but now and again…"

Now that he knew his way, Roanne stayed quiet, brooding about the multiple missed chances to have stopped Fedor before he killed Dodi, about her own and Nolan's near disaster, about the kiss that had probably ignited because of the tension. Thank goodness the other agents had surrounded the house. Still, her gaze kept wandering to Nolan's hands and powerful forearms. She couldn't deny that she'd loved holding hands with him, whatever his intentions.

At last, she forced herself to focus on her job.

They had almost reached the pockmarked road when

she said, "There's another woman we should talk with. She's the principal of the elementary school. She probably was responsible for the multiple reports to CPS. She testified about earlier abuse and about a conversation she'd had with Dodi a couple of days before the girl was killed.

"She told me Dodi was scared and inarticulate. Her head hung, and she hid behind her hair. The principal did note that Dodi was developing a figure despite being only ten, but she wouldn't say whether any man, friend of her mother or neighbor—or cult leader—had said or done anything with a sexual connotation. She had to explain what she meant, and Dodi hunched into a ball. She planned to have one of the case workers speak to her and her mother. The last thing the principal said on the stand was 'I'll never forgive myself for not taking her away that day.' I shared the regret. The problem is we have to step so carefully. We can never act as fast as we'd like." Roanne swallowed. "Tears were running down her face."

"You're right," he said quietly.

The community appeared as deserted as it had the last time they'd been there. "Let's look for Dodi's mother. If we have to, we'll knock on every door."

Roanne nodded. "Hers was that trailer nearest the lodge…" Her voice trailed off when she saw broken windows and vines growing into the trailer. Nolan braked, and they both got out.

He circled the trailer and shook his head as soon as he reappeared. "Nobody has lived here in a long time."

"I would have moved if I was her."

"She died," said a harsh voice behind her.

Chapter Thirteen

Somehow Nolan knew before they turned that it was the same man they'd spoken to last time.

"I'm sorry," Roanne said gently.

She was capable of more compassion than he could feel right now.

"Killed herself. Once the trial was over, what did she have left?"

Nolan knew he sounded just as hard. "I'd be more sympathetic if she'd tried to save Dodi."

"How do you know she didn't?"

"Several people spoke to Dodi during the couple of days before she was beaten to death." Roanne met the grim stare. "Did she not say to her mom, *Fedor wants to do something bad to me*?"

"Was it bad? He loved all of us."

Nolan snorted. "Beating a kid to death isn't my idea of love. Hurting a bunch of the other kids is almost as bad."

That voice cracked. "We...some of us tried to tell him he was going too far."

Unconvinced, Nolan planted his hands on his hips, one close to the butt of his gun. "We haven't found any records regarding Shelly Smith's death. Was that not her name? Where is her body?"

The man jerked his head toward the nearest stand of too-dry evergreens. "We've got a cemetery. None of us would want to be buried beside the unfaithful."

He hesitated, then led them to a dry clearing. In place of traditional headstones, chunks of concrete had been placed on what were presumably graves, names scratched on them. Many of those names were illegible. He nodded at one, where *S. Smith* barely was readable. "Only name I knew."

Nolan counted. The concrete marked ten graves. Considering what a relatively short time the cult had thrived here, that was a lot of dead people.

"Are any of these children?"

"Don't rightly know. They'd be with their Lord now, and it might have been different if'n all you hadn't condemned us without knowing a thing about us."

"I saw Dodi's body," Roanne said scathingly. "Did you?" She didn't react when Nolan moved closer enough to her that his upper arm brushed hers. She also didn't seem to notice him pulling his phone from his pocket and glancing at a text.

The cult's defender hunched his shoulders and took a step back. "That all you wanted?"

"No," Nolan said. "We'll be back to talk to every person still living here."

Roanne's lips formed the word *back*.

"We got a right to privacy," this whiny piece of you-know-what claimed.

"Once you've murdered a child, you've lost any rights," Nolan snapped and laid a reassuring hand on Roanne's back after ensuring their guide walked ahead of them. He probably wasn't armed, but 'probably' wasn't good enough. "Don't get in our way."

ROANNE WAITED UNTIL they were closed in his vehicle before asking why they weren't thoroughly canvassing the community as they'd intended.

"Didn't you get a text?"

"I... No. Is it bad?"

"No, but I need to show my face." He watched her read the same text he'd seen. Larry Ferguson had reached out because he'd found a package in his mailbox that wasn't anything he ordered. He didn't think it had a return address, either.

Maybe I'm being paranoid, he'd told the 911 operator, *but I'd appreciate someone coming to take a look.*

Roanne closed her eyes in a moment of what looked like resignation before she said, "Ferguson was Fedor's lead defense attorney."

"The one who didn't get him off."

"Yes."

What else was there to say?

For the remainder of the drive, Roanne took one phone call after another, even as Nolan did the same with his Bluetooth. The first of hers, Nolan gathered, was from the police chief. Only half his attention on his own conversation, he tensed at the threat Brenk would try to pull her off this investigation, but Roanne first told him about the bombs rigged at her house and said, "I recognize I'm a target, but it's too late to prevent that." Pause. "Yes, I do, sir."

From his tone, Brenk then grumbled, and Nolan could guess why. He had seen the morning newspapers, with headlines that smacked of sensationalism: "Terrorist Stalks the Citizens of Rosendaal." Several complained that police weren't doing enough. Nolan even sympathized with that one; it was true that federal agents hadn't made any meaningful progress toward making an arrest.

Rosendaal had achieved online fame, too, but not the kind the city fathers wanted. A photograph of the shattered, burning remains of Curtis Whitley's front porch, the small, grieving child held by a kneeling firefighter, might've been the most looked-at image on the internet right now.

Roanne's next call was her dad. She became warm and reassuring. Of course she was safe. She hoped the agents he was putting up weren't too much of a bother. A new call came in even as she said goodbye.

Nolan was turning into the courthouse parking lot when Roanne dropped her phone into a cup holder and whimpered.

"I didn't think the mayor even knew my name."

Despite his grim mood, Nolan laughed.

PREDICTABLY, SHARON WAS DELIGHTED. Evidently, the tripwire bombs at Roanne's house had been of a simpler construction, while this one left in the mailbox appeared to be nearly an exact copy of the initial pipe bomb at the courthouse that she'd had to piece together. This one, carefully dismantled, gave her a blueprint to ensure her reconstruction of the first one was accurate. She'd even spotlighted why this one probably wouldn't have detonated even if the defense attorney had been foolish enough to grab it out of his mailbox.

Their bomber had made a mistake.

As always, Nolan set the machine into motion—some to check for bombs in any other mailboxes belonging to possible victims and others to canvass.

Privately to Roanne, he growled, "Somebody somewhere *has* to have seen this guy! Doesn't anybody pay attention if you see a person opening a mailbox when he's not the postman and the box isn't his?"

"Ferguson's house is as private as Curtis Whitley's was. That doesn't help. Although..." Her posture radiated tension. "Given everything that's happened, you'd think more people would pay attention."

Yeah, he would, but so far they were batting three and out.

"I want to go back to the commune," he said grimly. "Maybe I'm wearing blinders, but I believe that's where the answers are."

Roanne didn't disagree—or agree, but it wasn't as if they had any other strings to pull. So he repeated the drive on the all-too-familiar route and, despite his experience, dropped them into a few potholes that could have cracked a molar. Roanne, of course, didn't say a word.

The first trailer they passed had slumped off its cinder block foundation. Tilted as it was, even the front door was warped.

"Maybe we could bunk there tonight," Nolan said drily.

A dimple appeared in her cheek. "Looks cozy."

Nobody was home—or answering knocks—at the next three habitations, traditionally built or old trailer. At the fourth home, a log cabin in better shape than most, a woman opened the door. She looked so thin, Nolan wondered if she were malnourished. The room behind her appeared clean, and although she studied them, she didn't slam the door in their faces.

"What do you think you're going to find here?" she asked, voice raspy.

"Information," Roanne answered. "Fedor never married, did he?"

"We were all his wives."

"He must have left some children," Nolan said.

"We were all his children."

How touching. In a grand sense, Fedor had committed incest every time he claimed a woman.

"So now what?" Roanne asked. "You're still here."

A flicker of anger lit flat brown eyes. "Where would we go? Anyway, we have to hold on to faith."

"That Fedor will come back?"

"Maybe. Or—" She broke off as if alarmed by what she'd come close to saying.

"Or?" Nolan asked.

"Our business isn't yours." This time, she did shut the door firmly.

They heard the lock turn.

Roanne walked to the next trailer, while Nolan moved his SUV.

Nobody answered when she knocked, but she heard scrabbling and shushing sounds from within.

"We just want to talk!" she called. "Find out what we can do to help you folks up here."

She waited, the set of her shoulders indicating she was aware of his approach. People had accused him of sneaking around before, but being aware of how he was setting each foot down was a legacy of his military service. He'd learned how dangerous a giveaway creak or snap of a twig could be. Roanne seemed to hear or maybe just sense him when he'd swear he hadn't made a sound.

No surprise when his gaze went straight to her in a crowd. Probably even in the dark.

The door opened a crack. Two children peered out—one no more than five or six, the other a couple of years older.

Pity softened Nolan's face. "Your mom or dad home?"

"I'm the dad here," the older kid declared, his voice cracking.

From the sliver Nolan could see, both children were as skinny as ones he'd seen scrabbling for a living in poverty stricken parts of the world—and as those two boys he and Roanne had seen on their first visit.

"Do either of you go to school?" he asked.

The little girl shook her head. "They'd take me away from Eddie. I ain't going to let them do that."

"What if we promise they wouldn't?" Roanne said softly.

Would authorities honor that promise?

She coaxed them. "You'd get a free lunch every day and maybe breakfast, too. Plus you'd learn to read and do math."

"Don't know about that," the older boy said gruffly.

She smiled with a warmth Nolan let himself bask in, even if it wasn't aimed his way. "What if I pick you up some day to go talk to the school counselor? I promise I'll stay with you, if you're willing to go. I'll bring you home, too."

The two kids exchanged glances.

The boy shrugged. "I don't know."

He was wavering, though.

"You don't think Fedor is coming back, do you?" Nolan asked. "He's going to be in prison for a long time because he killed Dodi. Did you know her?"

The boy mumbled, "Yeah."

"Do you *want* him to come back?"

Both faces screwed up with doubt.

"Doesn't seem like he has any family," Roanne contributed. "I mean, except for the few people left here."

"We got an uncle," the girl claimed.

Her brother shushed her. "We're not supposed to say."

"How come? He said he'd take care of us when he's finished..." She trailed off, her face crinkled. "With something."

Nolan felt a moment of savage triumph.

"Have you met your uncle?" Roanne asked gently.

The girl straightened. "'Course we have."

"What's his name? Maybe I know him, too."

This time, her brother clapped a hand over her mouth. "He's not nobody's business but ours!"

Unsurprised, Nolan had heard the approach of the warm, friendly fellow whose role apparently included guard dog. Did he have eyes in the back of his head?

"You got no business talking to those kids without their ma or pa being there!"

Nolan turned, taking advantage of the extra height from a step, hardly needed given that he had six inches or more on this man.

"Doesn't sound like they have either a mother or father," he said.

"We take care a' them!"

"Do you?" Nolan probably sounded as scathing as he felt and didn't care. "They're skin and bones. They need adequate nutrition and schooling."

The girl's voice piped up. "Mama only died this year."

"Two years ago," her brother corrected.

"That's not your business!" the man exclaimed.

Nolan was getting tired of hearing that. "What's your name?"

The fellow backed up a step. "Why do you want to know?"

"Because you're claiming responsibility for these two children. What are their names? Do you live with them?

Are you homeschooling? Can you show me their vaccination records?"

"I'd like to see their kitchen," Roanne added, a stony glance aimed at the man. "Just to be sure they have plenty to eat."

"We're a little short sometimes. Hasn't killed us yet."

"No? Then what did kill all those people buried back in the woods? Or maybe I should say *who*." She thrust out her chin. "What killed these children's mother?"

His mouth opened and closed a few times as he retreated another step or two. "Don't know. I ain't a doctor."

"Here's what we're going to do," Nolan said. "I have a few groceries in the car. I'm going to give them to these children, and I don't want anyone else helping themselves. You hear me?"

His "Yeah" was sullen.

Nolan raised his brows. "We'll be back four days from now to take these kids, and any others in this neighborhood, to be enrolled in school."

"But how would we get there?" the boy worried.

"Once you're enrolled, the school bus will stop right there, before the turn into your neighborhood." Roanne pointed. "You've seen it go by before, haven't you?"

They nodded.

Nolan went to the back of his SUV and plucked out a bulging grocery bag, bringing it back to the kids. "Does your stove work?" he asked.

The boy nodded as he craned his neck trying to see what was inside the bag.

"How about your refrigerator?"

"I'll fix it," the man behind him said. "I think I can."

"Okay. We'll check when we come back. If you need

parts, call me." Nolan handed over a business card. "Now I want your name."

The rottweiler of the neighborhood looked smaller, somehow, than he had the first time he confronted them. His shoulders rounded, his expression...sheepish, Nolan decided.

"Andy Spooner. Been here since the beginning."

"The children?"

"Annie and Eddie."

"Tell me about their uncle."

Alarm tightened the skin around his eyes. "They're making up stories—that's all." He scuttled back. "I got fields to tend."

Roanne and Nolan both watched him rush away, stopping at one trailer to speak to someone briefly—he and the woman looking over their shoulders at the intruders—before disappearing.

Only two more people proved willing to speak to them at all, and both responded to questions in unhelpful mumbles. Only the second said anything of interest.

"Fedor promised a second coming. May not look like him, but he'd be himself in spirit."

Even she didn't seem to know quite what that meant, but Nolan had a bad feeling.

Once he and Roanne buckled themselves into his SUV, he started the engine but didn't immediately put it in gear. In fact, he sat with his wrists resting on the steering wheel. His brooding stare took in the entire semicircle of decrepit housing.

"I'm ashamed of myself," Roanne said suddenly. "Why didn't I ever come out here and *look*? This is like...like the Dust Bowl poverty."

"It's not your responsibility. It's hard to see when the

people still here live in intact homes and melt out of sight the minute an outsider turns in."

He could see she wasn't satisfied with his attempt to let her off the hook.

"I never imagined children were trying to scrape by on their own!"

Nolan grasped her chin and turned her head so she had to look into his eyes. "You can't take responsibility for everyone, Roanne. You know that. Where were the social workers? School authorities? Workers who should have been checking meters on the houses?"

She stared at him with quivering distress before letting her shoulders slump. "You're right. But I could so easily— If I'd come alone—"

"You know better than that."

"The food bank has a truck for hauling donations. I wonder if they'd come up here and park like the bookmobile to hand out food."

"Would people take it?"

Expression bleak, she said, "I don't know."

Still, they sat in silence for a minute. She was the one to say, "We need to figure out who the 'uncle' is. Did Fedor have a brother? Surely he wouldn't have named a successor who wasn't a close relation."

Voice hard, Nolan said, "I think we both know what job 'uncle' has to finish before he comes up here to revive the colony."

Chapter Fourteen

"We need to look harder at his background. It didn't seem relevant at the time of the trial. No one claiming to be family ever showed up. I looked again the other day—"

"I did, too," he murmured.

"He hasn't had a single visitor at the correctional institute."

"Phone records?"

"He used a throwaway that someone made disappear before we could get our hands on it."

Nolan bumped his head once on the seat rest, then fired up the engine. "All right. We know who we're looking for now, just not what identity he's taken on."

Slowly, she said, "We have to go back to our original list. Who could have planted the bomb on Judge Anderson's desk?"

He'd believed from the start that the courthouse bombing investigation offered their best chance of narrowing the list to the guilty party. "I have an idea about that, but we can't jump to conclusions."

"We can go back and talk to all of them again."

"I'll put someone else on digging into Fedor's history. He didn't appear here freshly sprung from the earth. It seems likely he'd have had contact with authorities somewhere along the way."

Roanne started to agree, but the front right wheel on the big vehicle descended into a pothole and her teeth snapped shut.

"Sorry." His hand caught hers for a quick squeeze. "Let's go back to town and do some reorganizing. Eventually, we'll have to decide where to stay tonight."

"Actually, I had an idea about that."

He raised his brows.

"The judge and his wife keep a good-sized camp trailer parked behind their house. Erik moved into it at one point, just to assert his independence. I think the electricity may be hooked up to the house, but if not, there's a propane heater and appliances."

He had his doubts, but they had no reason to think the bomber had looked over the judge's house, much less taken note of a camper parked in back.

"As long as we're careful that no one follows us…"

"We may want to pick up something for breakfast. And, well, toothpaste and what have you."

They both had duffels, but hers had been hastily packed and weighed considerably less than his. "We can do that," he agreed. "I had some emergency food supplies, but—" He shrugged.

Her smile radiated approval and something extra that tightened a knot beneath his breastbone. He shouldn't take advantage of the situation…but they'd certainly have privacy tonight.

Private thoughts got sidetracked when the police radio crackled.

911 OPERATOR: *"You say there was an explosion. Is this at home?"*

"Yes!" The woman sounded hysterical. "He just didn't think! He didn't think!"

"Who didn't think, ma'am?"

"My husband. He's...oh, God. I'm going to be sick."

A gagging sound was heard in the background as the dispatcher tried to calm the caller.

EVEN AS NOLAN and Roanne raced through town, lights flashing, they knew the bomber had struck at Theresa Bishop's home. Despite warnings, she and her husband had stayed put. This time, the bomber had missed his target, although Roanne had an angry suspicion that he wouldn't care. He'd hurt Theresa either way.

An ambulance and two police cars beat them to the home, a rambler on what might've been as much as an acre. Smoke rose as well as the acrid scent that Roanne hoped wasn't burning flesh.

Two medics were loading a patient into the back of their unit, moving with urgency. Was Theresa's husband alive?

Roanne jumped out as soon as Nolan came to a stop at an angle in the street to block traffic. She ran, seeing a distraught woman she barely recognized. Face wet with tears, Theresa wrung her hands in a way that had to be painful.

Theresa looked toward Roanne but not with recognition. She saw a person—that was all.

"We were packing. We were. Paul thought we were overreacting. But he knew! He knew!"

Roanne sensed she wasn't ready to collapse into an embrace. "What did he know?" she asked gently.

"Not to pick up a package. We knew the Whitleys,

you see, but…" A pretty woman with short, unashamedly gray hair, the social worker drew a shuddering breath. "The doorbell rang. He ordered a lot of books online. If the package had just been sitting there… But it wasn't. I heard the doorbell, saw him open the door and bend over." Overflowing eyes met Roanne's. "I didn't even have a chance to yell *No!*"

Nolan joined them, and when he reached for her, she flung herself into his embrace and cried on his chest. Over her shoulder, Roanne saw the anguish in his eyes.

"The husband?" she murmured.

"Burned but alive. Not what that—" He swallowed some language she agreed with. "Got the wrong victim, who may survive. He has to know he won't have another chance at Ms. Bishop."

"Depending…" She glanced cautiously at the grieving woman. "He may be satisfied."

Out of the corner of her eye, Roanne saw another woman hurrying across the lawn. Middle-aged, she didn't seem to notice her feet were bare.

"I'm the Bishops' neighbor. Lettie Wendell. I can take her home with me, or…" She lowered her voice. "I saw the ambulance. Is Paul, um…?"

"Yes. That's good of you," Roanne said. "Let me check."

Nolan said, "What I know so far is that Mr. Bishop suffered severe burns and will be transferred, probably by air, to a top-line burn unit in Seattle."

"Is there time for Theresa to get to the hospital and go with him?"

"I think so."

The neighbor glanced at her bare feet. "I need shoes, and then I'll drive her. If you can wait for a minute?"

"Of course. Thank you."

Three minutes later, they were on their way, and Roanne and Nolan had joined the ATF members who'd arrived as well as firefighters and other cops.

"It's midday," Roanne said, her throat feeling raw. "Did he want to be here to watch his own bomb go off? He took quite a chance that he might be seen."

"And this is three—no, four—bombs in one day," Nolan concluded. "Maybe he knows he's running out of time."

HE WAS IMMEDIATELY immersed in directing the likely futile hunt for a witness. If somebody had rang the doorbell, they would have had to disappear before anyone opened the door. Roanne wished Paul Bishop had been in any condition to answer questions. If a delivery truck pulled into the driveway or up to the curb, wouldn't he have been subliminally aware? A doorbell out of nowhere would make you more likely to expect a neighbor or the like on your doorstep, not a package on your welcome mat.

But the bomber had to get there and escape, so agents fanned out to canvass ten block or more each direction. Unfortunately, because the houses were on larger lots—between half an acre and an acre, at a guess—the odds were poor from the beginning that anyone would have noticed someone entering the Bishops' driveway. Also, this was the kind of neighborhood where most adults worked.

Roanne hitched a ride with one of the responding patrol officers and returned to the courthouse, where she occupied herself in a search of Fedor's background. Yes, Nolan had assigned the task to someone else, but she felt both angry and motivated.

She started by calling the school principal, who was a

logical next target, and urged her to take a vacation. She also discussed with her the hungry children she'd found at the compound and the possibility of enrolling them as soon as possible, to also receive free meals.

Mrs. Faber was receptive to the latter, while wanting to brush off any danger to herself. "How would he even know I passed on my concerns?"

"The same way he knew Theresa Bishop put the allegations together and went to the police."

The principal fell silent. "I'm so sorry to hear about Paul. What a ghastly thing to happen. She was going to retire in July. Do you know that?"

"No, I haven't had reason to talk to her recently. The fact that her husband wasn't killed instantly, like Curtis Whitley, gives me hope."

"By all means, bring the children," Trisha Faber said. "I don't see how we can get away without involving social workers, though. If they don't have a parent to sign for them…"

"Yes, I'm aware. I don't know how many children there are in the compound, but assume some do have a parent. The brother and sister I told you about…well, foster care is inevitable, but I promised they wouldn't be separated."

"We don't always get what we want."

Roanne shot back, "If I have to find someone willing to foster them myself, I'll make it happen."

She had appropriated Judge Anderson's chambers when she first arrived, confident he wouldn't mind. Hector Martinez, the agent assigned to the same search, found her there. Dark-haired and stocky, Hector appeared to be about her age.

"I found a Theodore Knepper," he announced, pulling up a chair to the desk and setting down his open laptop.

"School records. Idaho. Can't be sure this is our man, but Theo is catchier than Dwayne."

"I was stuck on Dwayne," she admitted. "Is Theodore this kid's middle name?"

"I think so." He showed her what he'd found and stayed in the judge's chamber while they both delved into what seemed to be a promising lead.

"The parent who enrolled him is Shirley Koster," Roanne mused.

Not a minute later, Hector said, "The father is listed as Ronald Knepper."

"Yes!" They shared a high five.

Shirley made next-to-no imprint on the internet. She'd listed *waitress* as her profession on school papers and claimed to be divorced. Fifteen minutes later, Roanne uncovered Shirley Koster's death notice. Brief as the few lines were, it remarked that she had had two sons and a daughter, the daughter having predeceased her. Naturally, the name of the second son eluded both Hector and Roanne.

"Different father," Hector said. "Has to be."

"I agree."

Shirley's name did not appear again as enrolling a second child in the school district, suggesting she'd moved.

They split up to make calls. Unfortunately, the odds were against them finding anyone in the small Idaho town who remembered a boy who'd attended school there thirty to forty years ago, but they had to try.

Employing a good deal of patience, Roanne reached a retired school principal with a creaky voice who said, "That family were with a commune right outside town. You know we've got a lot of that kind of thing in these parts. You may remember the Ruby Ridge shootout."

"I don't recall the details."

He told her more than she needed to know but transitioned back to Theo's family. "The kids mostly went to school. Don't know if they were poor or if every penny any of the parents had went to their leader. I can still see them in hand-me-downs that belonged in the rag basket."

Fedor's choice of establishing a commune of his own suddenly made sense.

The old man only vaguely remembered there'd been a second boy who maybe went to school there only for a year or two. The commune had broken up and most people moved. "Name stood out, though. He wasn't Tom or Gary or anything like that. Wish I could remember. I know he had a different last name. The girl was the oldest, and *she* had yet another last name." His disapproval was apparent.

Roanne gave him her phone number in case he recalled the younger son's name—or could think of anyone else who might know.

She and Hector agreed they'd come to a dead end at that point but were a step ahead.

NOT LONG THEREAFTER, Nolan appeared, knowing how ragged he must've looked. Sleep was a luxury during an investigation like this, but frustration had an aging effect, too. He probably did betray amusement at finding her ensconced in Judge Anderson's sacred chambers.

"Only the best for you," he said.

"He's Uncle Charles, remember? He wouldn't mind."

"I wondered," Hector said.

Nolan grunted, then asked for any update. They shared what they'd learned, which lightened his somber mood. "Good work, both of you."

"Is Theresa's husband still alive?"

"Last I heard. He's in the burn unit, but it looks like he turned away and protected part of his body. The worst damage is to his back and one side."

Roanne pressed her lips together and nodded.

"I'm starved," Nolan said. "Hector, you want to join us to get some dinner?"

Hector agreed, although he'd had lunch, unlike Roanne and Nolan. Nolan had always liked him, and despite the overall grim mood, he was a good choice for a dinner companion. He had a sly sense of humor that enlivened their booth at a downtown café. Nolan glanced around and noted that most of the tables and booths were occupied by federal agents, as probably were most sleeping accommodations.

At least the feds would pay their bills, which was the silver lining to the reality that tourism had taken a nosedive. The question was whether it would rebound once they made an arrest.

If, he thought, then shook his head. *No, when*.

They parted ways in the parking lot, Hector not asking where Roanne and Nolan were staying. Nolan nodded over his shoulder and said, "I made a quick grocery run. Pretty basic. I hope you like doughnuts and don't mind instant coffee."

"Not picky," she said. "You remember the way?"

Silly question.

As they drove through the increasingly dark night, Nolan studied his GPS and made several unnecessary turns and detours. Roanne didn't comment on his caution, especially after he mentioned an ATF agent had gone over his SUV with a fine-tooth comb in search for a tracker and not found one.

He made a few more remarks about his day and the

mass search for the bomber, but much of the way they drove in silence. A half-moon emerged from behind a cloud just as they reached the judge's long driveway. Nolan turned off the headlights, slowed down and maneuvered to the house. Roanne pointed out the unobtrusive lane that entered a stand of evergreens and emerged behind a sizeable camp trailer. It was with huge relief when he turned off the engine. He liked his job—he did, but the devastation they'd seen this past week made him feel like a failure. In a town as small as this, why couldn't they narrow down their pool of suspects? Tension rode his shoulders like the kind of weight he'd carried on his back in war zones.

"You need the headlights to find the key?" he asked.

"No, I'll just use my phone. Cross your fingers they haven't changed the hiding place."

They hadn't. A moment later, she opened the door to let them into a chilly, pitch-dark interior. Nolan made the rounds to check that all the blinds were tightly closed, then went outside to see how much light leaked out.

"Not much," he announced, coming back in. "I think we can use a light or two in here."

Roanne had already located the light switch for the living and dining area.

"This is pretty luxurious," Nolan commented, looking around. "If we can heat it up a little..."

As the heater hummed, they talked about their days, Nolan letting himself express his discouragement, something he normally wouldn't do. Roanne admitted to having felt a minor flashback when she'd gone upstairs to the floor where judge's chambers were housed.

"I don't know if they'll do anything to hide the damage. Or if they can! I mean, marble! There are chips all over."

"I noticed. Some of them were taken out of your flesh."

"Ugh." She made a face at him. "I haven't even looked to see if I'll have scars on my back."

He'd be happy to check for her. Nolan was beginning to think this isolated camper was either a good idea for the two of them to share....or a bad one.

Chapter Fifteen

Nolan was far more aware that the two of them were alone together than he'd been at her house, where neighboring porch lights and lampposts and occasional traffic had kept him aware they were in town.

"Let's figure out where we can sleep," he said abruptly, only then aware he'd interrupted her in the middle of a sentence. When he apologized, she said, "It wasn't important. I was filling the silence."

"I hope there's some bedding in here." The interior was warm enough now that it wouldn't be the end of the world if they had to curl up in their clothes. "If you want to look, I'll go out and get our bags."

The moment he stepped outside, he noticed how quiet it was. A hint of glowing sky lay to the east where town still hadn't shut down. Otherwise, he thought he heard the soft hoot of an owl and some rustles in the trees. He felt a prickle of discomfort. He wasn't sure he'd like living on acreage like this. He'd spent too much of his life in close quarters with other people. Even his childhood home had been situated right in the small town where the ferry landed on Bainbridge Island in Puget Sound. They had neighbors. Busy ferry traffic passing at predictable interludes.

Yeah, he could adjust to small-town life, but he wondered whether Roanne would hate living in a busy city like Seattle. He reminded himself that she had to have lived in the Seattle area while she worked for the King County Sheriff's Department, then growled at himself. He'd barely kissed the woman, although he wanted to do a lot more than that. He was getting way ahead of himself, although he'd never met a woman who drew him the way she did at first sight or matched him in determination and focus. The compassion she'd showed those scared children touched him. She might take her sense of responsibility for everything that had ever gone wrong too far, but it revealed the core of a woman he could trust.

He grabbed their duffels from the back of his SUV, as well as the sack of groceries, and closed the hatch door as softly as he could.

When he stepped back inside and locked that door, he didn't see her. Her voice came from down a short hall.

"I haven't found any linens, but there are a comforter covering the bed and a pile of blankets and other comforters. We won't freeze. Towels are in the bathroom, too."

He left the grocery bag on the short kitchen counter and followed her voice with both their bags slung over his shoulders. She stood squeezed between a bed that consumed most of the small room and a bifold closet door.

"This looks good to me," he said.

She cast him a glance that was shy enough to surprise him. "I can sleep on the padded bench behind the dining room table. You'll fit better on this bed."

Which was queen-size, he guessed. Built-in, it appeared.

He dropped his duffel. "Can't we share the bed?"

"Well... I suppose."

Yeah, shy. She might've been smart, bold, even aggressive as a cop, but it appeared casual sex was another story for her. Or even just sleeping with a man?

"Unless you're wide awake, I suggest we hit the sack." That was what his mom had always said. "Heaven knows how early we'll be roused tomorrow."

Obviously distressed, she said, "That soon? He's running out of victims."

"Is he?" Nolan sat on the edge of the bed. Not a bad mattress. The bomber wouldn't have forgotten *her*, and she must've known that. "How do we know? We predicted the Bishop woman would be hit, but there may have been other social workers who enraged Fedor. I assume he owns the property still, or was he forced to sell it to pay the attorney? Or did he feel cheated by a real estate agent? The possibilities are almost unlimited."

Knowing how far they were from putting this creep away darkened Nolan's mood again.

Roanne studied him. "You're assuming he stayed in touch with his…"

"Successor?"

"I was going to say 'brother.'"

"You're convinced it is the brother we're looking for."

"It fits," she said. "If Fedor had had a devoted, half-competent right-hand man to leave as heir, I think we'd know it by now."

"Nobody competent is running that compound," he growled, again picturing the malnourished children. He paused. "You couldn't talk the principal into hiding."

"I think…she's used to command. Someone told me yesterday that she's slated to become the school superintendent next year. She's probably thinking nobody would dare take her on. Or maybe she's just in denial right now."

Roanne shuddered. "It almost makes me wish she'd seen the devastation at the Bishop's house. And smelled—" She balked.

The burning flesh. That was what she didn't want to say, and he didn't blame her. Given his history, he was familiar with the smell, but it never was anything but sickening.

"Let's get ready for bed," he said gently. "There's nothing more we can do tonight. I have agents taking shifts to watch her house," he added.

"Oh, thank goodness!" She unzipped her bag, pulled out toothpaste and toothbrush and brushed by him without quite meeting his eyes.

Nolan dug out his own and waited his turn in the bathroom.

He wasn't surprised when he returned to the bedroom to find her still hovering, although she'd spread a second fat comforter on the bed so they could asleep atop the first one.

"I wish I'd brought more clothes." She was either fretting or delaying. "If I sleep in these, they'll be wrinkled."

"Why sleep in them?" Nolan matter-of-factly began to strip, piling his own clothes because he did have a couple of changes in the duffel. Everything he'd brought would be wrinkled tomorrow anyway, but he hadn't arrived in town with a full wardrobe. Only a few agents had access to an ironing board. He'd look worse than he did if he hadn't taken advantage of Roanne's washer and dryer.

She sneaked a look at him before nodding. Despite the instinct that wanted him to sleep closest to the door and therefore be able to protect her, he got into bed first. She wouldn't like feeling as if he'd walled her in. It wasn't as if either of them could get up on the other side of the bed.

"No pillows," he realized. "Why don't you throw me one of those extra blankets and we can make a long pillow out of it?"

She did as he asked, then hastily finished unbuttoning her shirt, leaving herself in a pretty basic bra—no black lace here—and panties. She didn't need fancy lingerie, not with that body and the fire in her hair. She was beautiful: shapely, long-legged, yet taut with muscle in the right places. Just as well he was already under the comforter so she couldn't see how he was reacting.

Nolan held back her side of the comforter invitingly. Looking shy again, she slipped in. Neither had yet reached up to flick off the light.

He lay still for a minute. Words seemed safer to him than reaching for her and having her recoil.

"I want you," he said bluntly, even as he knew he was probably blowing it.

"What?" She rolled to face him. "I'm handy, so you're in the mood?"

"Is that really what you think?" He couldn't help being offended, even though the two of them knew each other bone-deep in one way, not at all in another.

"How am I supposed to know?" she cried. He hadn't flicked off the light yet and could see wariness that verged on fear in her eyes. "You must travel a lot. Maybe you pick up a woman every time you're stuck for weeks at some location."

Nolan's jaw ached from gritting his teeth, but, face it, this whole discussion was his fault.

"No," he said. "I'm famous, or maybe I should say infamous, for going into a zone when I'm on a job. Tunnel vision. If it's not about the investigation, I don't want to hear about it. In fact, it's been..." For a moment, he couldn't remember.

He'd gotten tired of going through the rituals required to get a woman in bed, and one-night stands with someone who was just a body didn't appeal to him. His parents' marriage had turned him off the idea of promising forever to someone, of being stuck with them or ditching a commitment, but right this second, he could easily see coming home to Roanne every day.

"A long time," he finished his sentence. "You're...different anyway. That night when you were in the hospital... You got to me. I didn't want to leave you in the morning."

Roanne blinked at him a few times, the glint of gold in her brown eyes somehow enhanced. Her auburn braid had slid down to create a sort of necklace.

"I didn't want you to go, either," she admitted, voice soft. "You were...my anchor."

He wanted to keep being her anchor, but this was too soon to say that. She might yet disappoint him, although he didn't believe it. As it was, he waited, muscles tight.

Then her mouth curved, just a little uncertainty still on her face, but she wriggled closer to him and said, "I want you, too."

He flipped to his side so he could kiss her.

NOLAN'S MOUTH ON hers lit a fire in her body like nothing Roanne had ever experienced. She'd be humiliated if he had the slightest idea how she'd watched him, fixating on his big, capable hands, one of which had already found her breast.

Her bra disappeared. She arched at his touch and slid her own hand under his white T-shirt. He was hot, his skin smooth, muscles jerking as she reached them. The hair on his chest was silky. She rubbed her palm on his flat nipple, and he groaned, then lunged to a sitting position so he could strip off the shirt. It went flying, and she had a second to admire the kind of body she'd never seen up close before.

"Wait!" she cried when he lay back down, half covering her. "I want to see—"

"Later."

At least, that was what she thought he'd said. His hands kept moving, kneading, stroking, teasing, and she could do little but clutch his powerful shoulders and answer his kiss with her own tongue and lips and teeth. She'd never felt anything like this; with her couple of semi-serious boyfriends, sex had been pleasant at best. This had her mind shutting down, while she tried desperately to pull him on top of her. She wanted him over her more than she'd ever wanted anything—him between her thighs, pushing, locking them together.

Savoring wasn't a possibility. This felt like she'd been caught in an ocean wave, tossed until she didn't know up from down. Yet he was never rough; the hands that moved her to suit him were always careful.

Just as he'd always been with her in every other way, she realized, the thought crystalizing.

He tossed her panties, then stroked between her legs, his mouth following. Roanne heard herself crying out, wanting more, tugging at him. She got her fingers beneath the waistband of his shorts, and he took over the task of getting rid of those, too.

Finally, he was there, the pressure at her opening almost agonizing as she waited for him to *move*.

Instead, he groaned. "Wait. I have to find a condom."

"I'm on birth control."

For an instant, he went still. "You're sure?"

"Yes!" She flattened her feet on the mattress and pushed up just as he thrust hard and deep. Nothing in her life had felt so good.

Nolan rocked her until all her tension sprang loose like a compressed spring, and then he let himself go, too, throbbing inside her.

When his weight came down on her, she held him tight, not wanting to ever let him go, even as she was stung with the hope that this wasn't the biggest mistake she'd ever made.

NOLAN HAD HAD his share of women over the years but had never felt like this. He was probably crushing her, but he was as hungry to continue feeling their bodies in full contact as he'd been at the beginning. His hips moved without any conscious decision, and when she arched in response, he found himself making love to her again.

They went slower this time, until near the end when he lost it and thought she did, too.

This time, he did reluctantly roll to his side, although he gathered her snugly against him. With her head on his shoulder, he could rub his jaw against her fiery hair and smile at a faint scent of lemon.

"You okay?" he asked.

"Better than okay. I've never—" Roanne broke off what she'd been about to say.

I've never, either, he couldn't help thinking. Too soon to say.

"I feel guilty, though." She rubbed her cheek against him. "I mean, that awful scene was today! Even if he survives, Paul Bishop will never be the same."

"No. But maybe we needed a release from the tension that's gripped us since the first bomb went off."

She stiffened. "That's what we were doing? Can't go to the gym, so we found another way to release tension?"

Nolan gave her a shake. "You know that's not what this was about. I'd have wanted you no matter how and when I met you. The idea that this piece of slime is still determined to hurt you scares me to death. I'd do anything—"

She pressed a kiss to his throat. "I…feel the same, you know. I'm glad you're not with the ATF. I don't think I could stand to see you defusing a bomb when the risks are so high. How *did* you do it?"

He cupped her breast giving himself both comfort and sensual pleasure. Voice gruff, he said, "I saw the results, over and over, of troops who'd been hit by an IED. Men and women, torn apart. A lot of those devices were more powerful than what we're seeing here in Rosendaal. If you'd been that close to one of them…" A shudder rattled him.

She tightened her hold on him and rubbed her cheek on the hollow below his shoulder. "I'm glad you don't have to do that anymore."

"You and me both. I don't want you to have to do any gymnastics to avoid getting blasted again, either."

She smiled. "Athletics, not gymnastics. I'm way too tall to be a gymnast."

"I like you the way you are."

The stress that had gripped her muscles all day—all week—had disappeared, leaving him utterly relaxed. His mind flicked to tomorrow, but he refused to let herself start worrying again. Instead, he sank into sleep, feeling Roanne doing the same.

THANK GOODNESS, THEY weren't roused early the next morning by a panicky 911 call. Maybe their target needed time to construct more devices. He'd certainly deployed enough in less than a week.

Roanne and Nolan had slept late enough. Nolan kissed her and then grumbled, "I'd like to take another half hour or so, but I don't think we dare."

She laughed at him despite the fact that she ached to be enveloped in his arms again. Instead, they scrambled into their clothes—yes, wrinkled—and left their duffels on the bed.

Even as they boiled water for their instant coffee, Roanne urged Nolan to check on Paul Bishop.

A minute later, Nolan reported, "He made it through the night, but with such severe burns, he's going to have a long haul ahead of him."

She'd *seen* those burns and was shocked that he hadn't been killed. Her stomach gave an uneasy stir. Severe burns were excruciating. Right now, he might've wished he *had* died.

Nolan got back on the phone only to be told there had been no activity in the vicinity of Mrs. Faber's home, which was mere blocks from the Bishops'.

While they ate doughnuts, Roanne said, "If you'll drop me at my car, I may do a big grocery shop and take the food up to the commune. It's possible someone could open up more."

"Let's go together," he said. "I don't know that I can add a lot to the investigations I've assigned, and I agree with you. I don't like picturing those kids, and some of the people who live there *must* know Fedor's heir."

She nodded. "After that, we should revisit some of the

people who were in the courthouse the day the package bomb was left for Judge Anderson."

"Blaine Weightman."

"He's at the top of my list, but I'm not sure we've looked hard enough at some of the other people we know were there that day. Blaine's assistant, for example. He's probably too young to be the brother, but we shouldn't get stuck on the idea of a brother. That assistant—whose name I can't remember—could be a son."

"There was a newly hired guard who made me uneasy."

Roanne knew who he was talking about, but the guy hadn't made any strong impression on her. She couldn't remember his face.

"I agree," she said. "Although would he have a background to give him the expertise he'd need to build bombs successfully?"

"Who knows." He frowned. "Hector was assigned to look into the histories of almost everyone we or anyone else talked to. The sheer numbers may mean he's still at it. One of the most frustrating aspects of this investigation is the lack of suspects tied to any of the other bombs. Nobody seems to have caught even a glance of a vehicle or person who didn't belong. What are the odds of that?"

"Sneaking around a house isn't that hard," Roanne pointed out. "Especially during the night. I do have trouble picturing why nobody at all saw anyone ring the Bishops' door bell."

Roanne guessed she wasn't the only one who suspected that somebody had, in fact, watched events once the doorbell had rung. Someone without the capacity to feel horror at what he'd done.

Chapter Sixteen

As they tidied up, she asked, "Can you keep watchers around Mrs. Faber's house over the weekend?"

"A schedule is already in place. I wish the school year were over."

"You don't think…?"

"I don't know." Some of the lines on Nolan's face deepened again. "I'd like to think this guy has some semblance of a conscience, but he didn't seem to worry about whether Curtis Whitley's little girl could have been the one to pick up the package."

"No. Just to be on the safe side, I'm going to call the principal again and ask her not to allow any maintenance of office equipment for the present, no matter how essential it is."

"And she should call if any mail and packages that don't have a clear and familiar return address arrives."

"Right."

Roanne had a feeling she'd gotten Mrs. Faber up, but she listened to the cautions—or call them orders—and agreed immediately.

"Although surely no one would bomb a school!"

"Let's just be extra cautious." Did she sound too soothing? Roanne worried.

"You're still bringing those children Monday morning?" the principal asked.

"That's the plan. And any of the parents I can round up, too."

"They are all elementary age?"

"So far as I've seen. I'm not positive about the two boys I saw the first time I went up there, but my best guess is they're fifth or sixth graders."

"We'll get it straightened out."

After hoisting herself into the passenger seat of Nolan's big vehicle, Roanne said, "I may have forgotten how to drive."

He flashed a grin at her. "Hey, you were on your own for part of yesterday."

It was true. What she couldn't let herself say was, *I'd have rather been with you.* Besides, she hadn't driven herself. In fact, she had trouble remembering the last time she'd seen her car.

NOLAN WOULD HAVE been willing to kick in money to fill some of the potholes leading into the compound. So far as he could see, though, there were only five vehicles, and one that sat without tires on cinder blocks that might once have been part of a mobile home foundation, while another appeared to have been in a head-on collision.

He and Roanne had loaded the back of his SUV with bags of groceries, enough to leave at least one bag at each household. The second door they knocked on turned out to be the home of the two skinny boys they'd seen on their first visit.

A woman behind them didn't look any better nourished than they did, but she snapped, "We don't take charity."

"You have children," Roanne asked.

She stared at them, then closed her eyes as if she were in pain. Or experiencing shame?

"I...yes. These are my boys."

"Are you letting them go to school when I pick up other children Monday?"

"Andy—my husband—he's going to take them. He thinks you're right they need to go to school." She sucked in a breath and reached out for the bag. Snatched it. "Thank you."

"Do you know—" Nolan started to ask. "That went well," he said to the closed door.

"She took the food, and Andy is going to bring their sons on Monday. That's encouraging. I've had the feeling he's sort of running the show here these days."

"You're right." What they were doing felt right, but Nolan couldn't let himself forget the urgent need to identify the bomber before anyone else died.

They received no answers as they made the rounds, but most people took a bag of groceries. Nolan left one on the porch of a trailer that appeared occupied even though no one came to the door, and they gave Eddie and Annie two that happened to include a few candy bars. Roanne reminded them what time she'd arrive to pick them up Monday, and they nodded with what might be cautious hope.

"You talk to the people at the food bank?" Nolan asked as they left, zigzagging to avoid as many potholes as possible.

"Yes. They need to discuss it, but the woman I spoke to was shocked to hear about this level of poverty. I think they'll do it."

"At least one good thing has come out of this," Nolan said.

Upon reaching town, they managed to get lucky and

catch Blaine Weightman's younger assistant loading a van behind the office.

Tall and gawky, his expression when he saw them made Nolan think of a shying horse. Too much white in those eyes.

Nolan held out a hand. "I know we met briefly, but we're making the rounds again, and I'm afraid I don't remember your name."

"I'm Joel Dietz. I don't know what I can tell you. I didn't see anything that day. I mean, I would have said if I had."

"It's not quite accurate to say you didn't see anything," Nolan said easily. "You must have seen a dozen people or more, maybe talked to a few of them."

He twitched. "Well, yeah, but that's because I was doing work for them."

"Did anyone hold open the back door for you and Blaine when you brought that desk in?" Roanne asked.

"I think so, but I didn't know him. He's a security guard—that's all I remember."

Keeping the conversation as relaxed as possible, Roanne and Nolan talked him through his day. He got even more nervous when he had to admit he lived alone, and worse yet, he'd majored in mechanical engineering in Washington State University before dropping out at the end of his junior year. "I just didn't fit" was his explanation.

"So how'd you end up taking this job?" Nolan asked.

"Well… I'm from Montana. Missoula, and I'd met Blaine there. He told me what kind of business he wanted to own and asked if I would be interested in moving and working for him."

"You've been here in town since he bought the business?"

"Uh-huh. Like, a couple of weeks later. My mom was mad I didn't finish my degree, and she said I had to do *something*. And... I said I'd go back to school eventually."

Would the university accept a student who'd dropped out of a prestigious program?

"How did you meet Blaine? He's got to be ten years older than you," Roanne asked.

"He rented an apartment over our garage for a while. He was working construction, and the way he talked about it I thought I might try it, but... I'm kind of clumsy and I've never worked out or anything, so I figured it may not be for me."

"Did he ever do demolition?" Nolan tried to sound casual.

"Demo...?"

"Blowing up a building that had to go before new construction, or blasting some rocks out of the way."

Enthusiasm shone on Joel's face for the first time. "He let me watch once when they took out some boulders to make a lot bigger. It was cool to see! Except," he hastened to add, "not if someone's hurt like that. It was just...interesting."

Interesting. The trouble was if you had no experience with explosives, it might *be* just that.

Joel seemed to have forgotten Roanne was there. That was fine with Nolan.

"You know anything about Blaine's family?" he asked.

There was a tiny pause before Joel shook his head. "I don't really know, except he didn't sound like it had been *good*. You know?"

"Never mentioned a brother?"

"No. Except..." The young man's forehead wrinkled. "He did say something about maybe having family here, although if he does, he's never talked about it."

"You know where he's working today?"

"It's Saturday," Joel said. "We're not that busy on weekends, so we take turns covering Saturdays. Sundays, we're just closed. You know, unless a really good customer has an emergency."

"Did he have plans this weekend?"

"He likes to fish...."

Nolan shook his hand again. "I'd appreciate it if you wouldn't mention talking to us. I'm guessing he wouldn't be happy to hear we're back to bug everyone."

"No, I won't. There's no reason to," Joel said with what might've been relief.

"Interesting," Roanne said once she'd hoisted herself back into the SUV seat. "I'd think that meant something, except I just can't picture Joel Dietz manufacturing bombs and sneaking around at night."

"The engineering background is a red flag."

"Yes, but..."

Nolan shrugged. "If he's our guy, he should have moved to Hollywood and become an actor."

Roanne laughed. He loved the sound—and what humor did to her already beautiful face.

He made calls, discovering that Blaine Weightman's receptionist didn't work Saturdays either; the call was answered by Joel. Nolan and Roanne drove by Blaine's rental house, which was the size of Roanne's but a lot shabbier. It, too, had a detached garage, but the two small windows were covered with bamboo shades, and the large door didn't give way to his hand. Not that he'd have opened it, tempted though he was. If Blaine Weightman was their man, Nolan wasn't about to foul up by violating the law.

He hammered on the front of the small house but got no answer. The second white van emblazoned with the name of the business had been parked right beside the one Joel had been getting out of. Blaine was registered as owner of an older gray Camry. That locked garage made Nolan nervous. It would be a perfect workshop.

"Blast it!" he exclaimed before grimacing. "Bad pun."

"Really bad," Roanne agreed, not even looking amused. "I wish he'd been home. Even without a warrant, it would have been hard for him to refuse to let us see his garage." A moment later, she asked, "*Can* you get a warrant?"

"Based on what? We're suspicious? I will put a tail on him, too, whenever he shows up."

"If he's the bomber, he's going to be watching for a tail."

"The agency has some people who are especially good at that. It's worth trying."

When he reached over and took her hand, she smiled at him even though her eyes remained dark and worried.

BLAINE WEIGHTMAN HAD done a vanishing act, at least through Sunday night when the aggravated agent assigned to locate him called Nolan. Roanne was able to listen because he had put the phone on speaker.

"Late afternoon today, I made myself more visible and chatted with a couple of neighbors," Agent Allworth said. "Neither of them seemed to know Blaine well. He bought chocolate a middle schooler was selling as a fundraiser, that kind of thing, but mostly kept to himself. One did say he must have a workshop in the garage, because they often see lights showing in the windows at night. He parks in the driveway."

Looking frustrated, Nolan said, "He's not registered as owning any other vehicle."

"I asked the more observant woman whether he didn't bring his company van home sometimes, but she said she'd never seen it there, just a couple of times around town."

Nolan swore before requesting he stay on it.

Roanne ended a call with Hector, who was still researching backgrounds of anyone who'd been at the courthouse that day. He mentioned that the newly hired security guard had grown up in Mount Vernon, just up the freeway, and had worked for a company that supplied security within the county. Hector had talked to him briefly, and he said he liked the stable hours better. A call to the former employer awakened surprise and curiosity—which Hector didn't satisfy—and a solid review.

"He never was likely," Nolan said when Roanne repeated what she'd learned.

"If Weightman isn't hunched in his garage making new bombs, where is he?" Frustration sharpened Nolan's voice.

She shook her head. "I say we give it up for the day and get some sleep. Do you know how early I have to pick up those kids?"

"Not you. *We*. And you told me." The corners of his eyes crinkled in a smile that didn't reach his lips. "Early to bed suits me fine."

She rolled her eyes but didn't argue. Depending on how many of the kids she had to transport, it could be a squeeze in her much smaller car. Plus, she found the atmosphere at the compound eerie. She wasn't afraid, but she always felt as if someone was watching her. No, she *knew* she was being watched. Cop or not, alone there she'd be more vulnerable than she liked.

Besides, she could hardly wait to slip into Nolan's arms, slide her hands over his powerful back, see the tenderness and heat on his face when he pushed inside her.

Just the thought made her thighs squeeze together. She felt quite sure Nolan noticed.

The night was as good as every other one since they'd started sharing a bed. Roanne had had no idea her body could be so responsive. He'd reassured her when he'd insisted that he didn't get involved with a woman in every port of call. To the contrary.

That didn't mean he would have any interest in extending their relationship, once this investigation was tied up. In most ways, Roanne wasn't timid, but she had less confidence in her appeal as a woman than she did in her competence on the job. She'd blamed her profession for her skimpy experience with relationships, but maybe the problem was with *her* and had nothing to do with how men reacted to her carrying a gun while she worked.

Maybe, like her father, she'd changed after the trauma of losing first her mother, then her brother. Or maybe she just hadn't met the right man.

She did know she wasn't going to be the one to say anything to Nolan about the future. Really, that would be ridiculous, given what a short time they'd known each other.

A voice in her head whispered to her. *Think about how many hours you've spent with him. How many meals you've shared. How he told you how scared he was for you.*

No matter what, she was being premature. They had to locate the bomber before anyone else got hurt.

Chapter Seventeen

Roanne was pleasantly surprised to find the five children ready to go and dressed in clean clothes that wouldn't stand out too much from what other kids wore. Andy Spooner owned a shabby but drivable pickup truck and intended to take his two. A child she'd been told about came out with her mother, a worn woman who asked anxiously if Roanne and Nolan could give her a ride, too.

"Andy says we should send them. I can get home with him," she explained, "but he doesn't have room for me along with his kids."

"Of course we do," Roanne said warmly. "I haven't met you."

She introduced herself, and the woman said haltingly, "I'm Jennifer Meechan, and this is Kelsey." Her hand lingered for a moment on her daughter's dark hair.

Roanne told herself she was imagining a resemblance between the girl and Fedor. Nolan looked from the girl to her, though, the same speculation in his eyes.

None of the kids said a peep during the drive back to town. Roanne turned to smile at all of them several times and once said, "You'll like Mrs. Faber, the principal at the elementary school. She always eats breakfast with the early arrivals."

Not even Jennifer Meechan seemed reassured. Roanne wished she knew whether any of these kids could read or write. Surely they'd be tested before being assigned to a classroom. And wouldn't these parents have done some homeschooling? They had to know that otherwise they'd be holding their children back!

Truthfully, she was as nervous as any of them, wishing she could be sure she was doing the right thing. What if other students made fun of these kids for being different? Children could be cruel. Would they get the extra tutoring and support they were bound to need?

Nolan parked as close to the main entrance to the school as he could, Andy pulling in next to him a minute later. Most students wouldn't arrive for another half hour, Roanne was reasonably sure.

They were greeted with smiles by the two women behind a counter at the entrance. "These are our new students?" one of them said, beaming at the children. "I'm so glad to meet you."

In the end, Roanne hastily filled out forms for Eddie and Annie with the understanding that at some point today, a social worker would come to talk to them. Otherwise, she and Nolan left Jennifer and Andy to register their kids.

Roanne held out a hand to Annie, who gazed at it for a moment as if she didn't understand why but finally laid her own hand in Roanne's.

There were plans—more like hopes—to build a new elementary school, but so far the bond issues hadn't passed. That left Mrs. Faber to deal with an occasional roof leak, condensation that clung to windows and a worn linoleum floor. Around ten years ago, the cafeteria had been added at the end of one wing by attaching two portables together.

They were linked to the old building by a roofed walkway. One served as kitchen, the other had seating for about half the students at a time. Roanne didn't like that the door she was ushering the children through was the only exit from the cafeteria. And okay, that was not a normal thing to worry about, but she preferred to foresee problems.

She'd already told Nolan she wanted to stay for as long as Mrs. Faber would put up with her. Certainly to eat with the kids, and maybe observe the testing. Determined to find Blaine Weightman, Nolan had agreed to come back for her when she called.

He introduced himself to the principal, then nodded to Roanne. After he walked out, the door leading to the walkway swung shut on its own. The setup made sense in one way: The racket from each shift of kids eating lunch wouldn't drift down a hall to disturb students who were still supposed to be concentrating on their classwork.

With the exception of Annie, the kids from the compound stayed shy but ate scrambled eggs, bacon and toast as if it were the best meal they'd ever seen. Mrs. Faber's eyes met Roanne's, pity in them. An angry part of Roanne wanted to believe the educators in this town should have been aware of these children who'd been forgotten, assuming they'd ever been on anyone's radar.

The principal apparently had already eaten and instead wandered among the tables to smile and touch the shoulders of the twenty or so kids who were here. Most of those chattered without inhibition to a woman who exuded warmth. Roanne felt encouraged by the interactions.

Mrs. Faber ended up at the table where Roanne sat with the new students. "I believe we'll do our testing here," she said. "I'm sure you're aware how short we are of space in this building."

"I vote yes on the bond issue every year," Roanne assured her. She understood people's budgets were tight but wished she could parade each and every one of them through this shabby building.

One of the cafeteria ladies started gathering the trays and dirty dishes. Glancing up at her, Roanne thought for a minute she'd seen a shadow pass in front of a window but decided she'd imagined it. Portables—at least older ones like these—had few and small windows. Besides, it was Monday. Especially with it now being spring, things like mowing and weeding and raking the bark under the climbers must be done sometime.

One of the front office staff showed up with a pile of papers and a bunch of pencils clutched in one hand. She smiled at everyone again and said, "Well, let's see! Who's new?" although she must've already known.

Annie raised her hand. "I'm new."

Roanne couldn't resist hugging her. The little girl even smelled sweet, which suggested she and her brother did have running water in their dilapidated home and they knew how to keep themselves clean.

With the principal's thanks, the front office woman departed, also letting the door swing shut behind her. Just before it closed, Roanne heard her say, "Oh, hello! Did you check in up front?" There was an odd sound that had Roanne dashing for the door before it latched.

Even though she'd expected something off, she didn't really think she'd find herself mere feet from Blaine Weightman. Out of the corner of her eye, she saw the plump older woman lying unconscious to one side.

Blaine's eyes narrowed on her. "You?" A cardboard box with closed flaps sat at his feet. Then he grinned.

She slammed the door in his face, which wasn't easy

since it wanted to move at its own pace. Then she leaned against it in hopes of keeping it closed.

Gasping, she heard the arrival of the first school bus. Oh, no! The building would soon be swarming with young students.

Her phone rang. Nolan's number came up. She answered, probably sounding hysterical. "He's here!"

"Weightman?"

"Yes!"

He said tautly, "I passed a van on the way back into town. Tan, a little battered, with tinted windows. When I braked to turn around, it sped away and I lost it. He had to be heading for the school."

"I think he met an office worker and knocked her out. I closed the door, but there's no lock. I wish I'd brought my gun in." Strictly verboten in a school. "Let me check to see if he's gone."

She turned the handle slowly, feeling as if the metal was burning her hand. The handle did turn, but the door didn't budge even though it was supposed to open inward. Blaine had to have wedged something on the threshold.

And then there was that box.

"I can't open the door without pushing hard," she said into the phone.

"No," he said sharply. "I want you to have Mrs. Faber stop the buses from unloading and evacuate students and teachers that are already in that wing of the school. Lie. Tell her I'm probably overreacting but we can't afford to take chances. I'll be there in minutes."

He was gone.

She hurried to the principal, trying not to project terror that the kids might pick up on. "Can I have a minute?" she asked.

Mrs. Faber's eyes sharpened. "Of course."

Roanne relayed Nolan's orders.

"But what makes him think...?"

Roanne told her about the man she'd briefly come face-to-face with, the jammed door and the office worker sprawled on the concrete.

"It's me he wants."

"Probably, but I'm a target, too." Roanne suppressed her own fear. "He looked delighted to see me here."

"But it's not just us. We have nineteen students here and two ladies in the kitchen."

"I know. Believe me."

"I'd forgotten you were the one who saved Judge Anderson that day at the courthouse." She shook her head. "I shouldn't prattle. Let me make calls."

Roanne approached the door into the old part of the building again, and pressed her ear to it. Dismayed, she heard some high voices of arriving children, but Mrs. Faber was speaking urgently into her phone.

Almost immediately, Roanne heard an intercom announcement, although she couldn't make out the words. Either the intercom never reached these portables or office staff had been able to cut them off.

She turned to see that everyone in the room, from Annie to a plump, gray-haired cafeteria worker, had nonetheless turned to stare at her.

Was there any hope the children, at least, could go out one of the small windows?

NOLAN DROVE WITH dangerous speed, screeching to a halt at the cafeteria end of the building. The first thing he saw was a cardboard box set against the wall, right below a window. He flung himself out of his vehicle, leaving the door open, and ran around back. Another box. Another on the third side.

He raced to the covered walkway and saw feet showing at the corner of the building. A middle-aged woman, unconscious rather than dead. The noise of children being herded down the hall away from danger surrounded him.

Leaving the unconscious woman where she was, he crouched in front of the door and immediately saw that a wedge made out of some dense plastic had been punched into the narrow space beneath the door.

Nolan swiveled on his heels to look at the box pushed right up against the door. He pulled out his phone, then froze. Was he hearing a clock ticking? He held his breath, bent forward and confirmed his fear.

Yes, this bomber had gotten even more sophisticated if he'd set timers on the bombs. Maybe that was the only way he could put four or more bombs into place without risking his own life. Given the flimsiness of the portables, he'd already overkilled with the number of bombs. If they all went off, they'd obliterate cafeteria and kitchen.

Rage felt like a punch to Nolan's chest. It had been conceivable that this monster hadn't known there would be a young child at the Whitleys' home. But here? At an elementary school?

He swept his gaze around, locking on a man running along the edge of the woods that lay between the school and city streets. It was no more than twenty yards from where Nolan stood. That son of a— He cupped his hands and bellowed, "We know who you are!"

The figure paused, back still turned. If he had a gun... but Nolan didn't see one.

He took a few steps closer. "You know who's in that cafeteria? Annie and Eddie, Kelsey and two boys who call you uncle. Remember them? They thought they could trust you, but you've just killed them."

Blaine Weightman actually turned. Even from this distance, he looked shocked. His mouth opened and closed. If he were trying to say something, he couldn't get it out.

"Their first day of school," Nolan told him, then turned his back, dismissing the presence of the bomber. They'd catch up to him. He punched in the number on his phone. "Answer, answer," he growled, by the third ring.

"Nolan?" It was Sharon Krogan.

"Where are you?"

"At the lab in Everett."

Half an hour or more away.

"Send anyone you can who has experience defusing bombs. He's set at least four around the elementary school cafeteria. The one in front of me has a clock. They all may." Then he swallowed and said the part that devastated him: "Detective Engle is in there along with the principal and around twenty children."

Urgency edging into desperation, Nolan ran for his own vehicle and the tool kit he always carried. He knew he couldn't wait for help. Weightman had disappeared

I'd give almost anything for a hazmat suit.

And to have been delayed this morning, so Roanne and all those hopeful children would be outside with him instead of trapped inside.

HER PHONE RANG AGAIN.

"You're surrounded by at least four bombs. I haven't checked the roof. I don't think he could have gotten under the portables. God knows he's placed more than enough explosives." The strain in Nolan's voice made the hair rise on the back of Roanne's neck. "I can't tell you yet how or when they're set to go off, but I know the one at the door is on a timer. That scum didn't want to take a chance of it blowing before he put the others in place. I've got a call in to the ATF agents, and there's an unconscious woman out here, too."

"The woman from the front desk. She saw him. I heard her talking briefly to someone, telling him he had to check in. That's why I went to the door." She took a deep breath. "The windows..."

"There's a bomb set beneath all of them."

"Could children be lifted out the windows over the boxes?"

"Conceivably," he said. "But probably not the adults. Also...who knows when they'll go off?"

Roanne closed her eyes and pressed her forehead against a wall. "How long do we have?"

"Don't know. I haven't opened the box yet."

A different kind of terror had the hand holding the phone shaking. "Surely you're not the one to do it."

"Nobody else is here," he said grimly.

ROANNE COULDN'T LET ANYONE, especially the children, see how petrified she was. Without the slightest idea how long they had, she clapped her hands. "Before you start testing, we'll do something fun. We're going to build a fort with the tables."

Children cheered. The two cafeteria ladies stood-stock still, mouths hanging open. Mrs. Faber somehow found a smile and exclaimed, "What a good idea! Where shall we build it?"

Up against the wall separating the kitchen from cafeteria. It was the only one free of a bomb. Roanne didn't let herself think about the typical poor construction of portables. Her fifth grade class had been held in one. She remembered it all too well. In winters the portables had been inadequately heated, while June and September meant the students had roasted.

And then there was the question of the usefulness of the tables.

"How about the windows?" the principal asked her quietly.

"No. There's a box beneath every one of them. If there isn't a timer, we could maybe hand some kids out once backup arrives. The only thing is..."

"A bomb could go off right at that moment." Mrs. Faber squared her shoulders and lifted her chin as if nothing in the world was wrong. She raised her voice. "We'll use that wall as one side of our fort. Let's drag tables over there."

Roanne had no faith whatsoever in her plan, but it had the benefit of keeping everyone, especially the children, occupied. If whatever barrier they had time to construct saved even one life, it was worthwhile.

The kids jumped enthusiastically into this project. Table legs screeched on the linoleum floor, and the tables themselves thumped when turned on their sides. They dragged them into a three-sided square with room for everyone inside. Then Roanne had them folding the metal legs and doubling the sides. What she couldn't decide was whether to try to create even a partial top—or whether that would increase the risk.

Chapter Eighteen

Nolan hoped from the siren he heard that an ambulance was nearing, although he didn't love the idea of endangering a pair of medics even if he'd like to get the unconscious woman moved.

As it was, he dropped to his knees beside the box placed beneath one of the windows. When he bent forward, he heard a faint ticking and let some words rip he wouldn't normally use. If every one of these IEDs was on a timer, how could he guess what order they were set to go off?

The one against the door was the largest box, and from what Roanne had reported, Nolan had to believe that one had been placed last.

He couldn't afford to waste time, so he decided upon the one placed on the side facing the school entrance.

Like the larger one at the door, the flaps of the box were folded rather than taped shut. It was tempting to rip open the box, which guaranteed he didn't. He'd bet it had been rigged to explode if someone did that, timer or no timer.

He pulled a razor-sharp Swiss knife, sucked in a breath and used the tip to pierce one side of the box. Gently, he sawed with it, careful not to bump anything inside. Within a minute, he had a window that allowed him to see dynamite sticks bundled, matchbooks attached to the type of stopwatch used to time sporting events—and a wire leading upward. The stopwatch had been placed so that he couldn't see how many minutes—or even just seconds—remained on it. He dropped the knife and picked up wire cutters.

There were always choices, any of which could be wrong.

This felt like a flashback. Here he was, doing something he'd sworn he'd never do again. The black powder in dynamite could be volatile, but he chose first to sever the matches from the sticks. A bead of sweat ran down his forehead and stung one of his eyes. He looked down to be sure his hands were steady.

They were.

Nolan couldn't let himself think about Roanne or all those children who hadn't had many breaks yet in their lives.

He sliced through the first wire, then cut between the stopwatch and the matches as well. Unless there was something he wasn't seeing, that should do it. Adding the clocks was a new twist for Weightman, but this bomb was still simplistic compared to ones Nolan had defused in the Middle East.

But no less deadly.

A single stick of dynamite would do enough damage. He thought again, *Overkill*. Not his favorite choice of words.

He rapped on the window and saw Roanne turning. He summoned her with one hand, then jumped to his feet and ran for the next bomb.

So MUCH FOR the fragile fort, although she could tell that the adults would be able to squeeze through the window.

A man appeared just outside the window. He looked only faintly familiar but wore a polo shirt she knew was emblazoned with FBI on his back. She shoved it up despite its squeaky reluctance and called, "Line up, kids! This is an emergency exercise. One at a time, you'll go out the window. There's a gentleman here to help you."

The line formed raggedly, Mrs. Faber helping with a few words and kindly touches. Annie and her brother happened to be first. Roanne lifted Annie and handed her to the man who straddled a cardboard box right outside. He handled her slight weight deftly, set her on the grass and said, "Run to that school bus. Do you see it?"

Panicky, she looked over her shoulder for Eddie, but Roanne was already hoisting the boy and easing him through. He grabbed his sister's hand, and they both ran.

So many more kids. Roanne couldn't see into the box—didn't even try—but guessed they had no more than three or four minutes, if that, before one or more of the bombs exploded inward through the flimsy walls of the portables.

She hated knowing what Nolan had to be doing. Where were all those ATF agents in their protective suits?

"Next."

EVERY ONE OF THE bombs had a timer, but otherwise they were all different. He found a pipe bomb packed with black powder and nails in one. Had Weightman enjoyed experimenting?

What would he do now that he'd been identified?

Nolan wiped the thought from his mind, along with his awareness of a stream of children running full out toward a school bus at the edge of the parking lot where several adults and a handful of federal agents waited for them.

Kneeling, he saw that this third bomb had a tangle of

wires coated in different colors, meant surely to confuse anyone trying to defuse it.

A man garbed in white appeared beside him. "Sharon says you need a hand."

Ya think? Nolan didn't even look up to try to identify which ATF agent this was. "There are at least two more, maybe three. I didn't check the roof or any other part of the school. Somebody better do that. We may need to bring in a dog before we let kids back in the school."

He gently picked through the wires in search of which were decoys and which would send the signal to blow him up—and probably Roanne. The day was far from hot, but he was sweating as though he'd just run a 10K. *Never again*, he vowed, for the second time in his life.

He wanted a life with the first woman he'd ever really fallen for.

THE LAST CHILD went out the window. Roanne thought she might be able to make it, but none of the other women. The cafeteria workers stood clutching each other, tears running down their faces. She couldn't save herself at their expense.

The FBI agent right outside the window asked, "Anyone else?"

His voice was familiar, and she had a vague memory of him making a point in one of their many morning conferences.

She turned. "Trisha?"

The principal shook her head. "I wouldn't make it. Anyway, he wants to kill me. I can't save myself and leave behind hard workers and friends. But you're more agile. You go."

Roanne said quietly, "No."

"All right. I'm told we're at least halfway around the building. The safest place for you is that corner." He pointed toward a part of the kitchen portable.

"Okay." She and Mrs. Faber ushered the other two women into the kitchen. They all sat down, huddling together.

NOLAN FOUND HIMSELF paralyzed for longer than he liked. Blue wire? Red? Yellow? Or what about the one that was next to invisible—fishing line, he assumed.

He tore off the latex gloves he'd put on earlier. He needed to be able to *feel* his way. He heard a shout and froze.

"We'll take care of the one by the door," a guy in a hazmat suit said behind him. "You need a hand?"

Yeah, Nolan wanted to keep both his hands. He'd just seen the stopwatch in this box. Thirty seconds. It counted down. Twenty-nine, twenty-eight. This was maybe the first one set.

"No time. Get back!"

The guy took one look over his shoulder, cursed and took off at a run. Nolan gave himself just a couple of seconds to jettison the clutch of fear beneath his breastbone before he went with instinct. He'd seen others like this. Bombers almost always thought they were trickier than anyone else.

He snipped the fishing wire—and the hand on the stopwatch quit moving at exactly twelve seconds.

Now Nolan's hands were shaking, but he cut a couple more wires to be sure the bundled match books couldn't ignite anything. Then he got up and ran again, needing to see for himself that someone was handling that last, probably largest explosive device.

ROANNE HEARD A hammering sound from the door that led to the walkway. Her heart thudded in accompaniment. Did that mean someone was removing the wedge or whatever had kept the door from opening? If so—

She murmured a prayer, something she didn't do often enough. Did her dad have any idea what was happening at the school? If so, he must've been terrified. Everyone in town must've heard the multiple sirens and see flashing lights.

As the door swung inward, she summoned the dignity to support her profession. She held out an arm to usher the other women ahead of her. Even with the cluster of people in the walkway, some wearing those bulky getups, she saw only Nolan, whose eyes never left her. No matter how much she wanted to throw herself into his arms, too many people were watching.

The other women were enveloped in the crowd, medics asking questions, one of the two cafeteria ladies breaking down and sobbing.

Mrs. Faber said, "The children? They're safe?"

"Yes, ma'am," one of the men said.

School buses lined up at the curb, children crammed up to the windows to see what was going on. How much would they be told?

Not my decision, Roanne knew.

Nolan reached her. "Roanne," he said, his voice ragged. He gripped her hand painfully hard, but it was a good pain.

Mrs. Faber said, "Agent Cantrell, what should I do now? Allow the children to go to their classrooms? I can't send them home when many wouldn't have a parent there."

He cleared his throat. "See how many parents you can contact. I think you have to keep the rest of the children, but give us some time to be sure no other bombs were placed on school grounds. I'm quite sure you won't want to use the cafeteria, though."

"I'd be happy to send as many children home as possible. I'll call the president of our PTA for help, and she can put out the word." Head high, she hustled away.

Roanne couldn't tear her gaze from Nolan's face. It was furrowed with lines she'd never seen before, giving her a good idea what he'd look like twenty or thirty years from now.

"Did you have to defuse bombs?"

He grimaced. "Most of them." He nodded toward one of the white-clad figures. "Some ATF agents showed up in time to take care of this one. Assuming there isn't a surprise somewhere else."

"Did you say you saw Blaine?"

"Oh, yeah." His jaw tightened. "I didn't have time to go after him. I've got people looking for him. I told him that the children from the compound were in there, and he seemed shocked. I guess no one told him the kids were going to start school."

Mad, she said, "But it was fine to blow up a bunch of other children?"

"Apparently so."

"He seemed surprised to see me." She grimaced. "But pleased."

Before they had further chance to talk, Nolan's attention was claimed by multiple agents, ATF and FBI and... She couldn't interpret the acronym on one of the shirts. Trying her best to hide the fact that her knees were shaking, she started toward the first bus, the one to which the children in the cafeteria had been directed. Of course, she had to have a reaction after the crisis.

Halfway, she felt as if she'd walked into a glass door. Surely Blaine would be found quickly. That would wrap up the investigation. Nolan would be leaving. Would he stay even one more night?

Her radio crackled.

911 OPERATOR: *"SIR, WHERE ARE you calling from? You believe this was an explosion?"*

"Yes! It went up like a fireball!" The caller sounded excited and terrified both. "I've never seen anything like it. We need fire trucks. Please hurry!"

911 operator: *"To your knowledge, was anybody injured?"*

"I...don't know. If anybody was in there, they have to be dead."

911 operator: *"The address, please."*

Roanne recognized it immediately.

NOLAN AND SEVERAL ATF agents came running. He grabbed Roanne's hand and hauled her toward his SUV. While others stayed behind, the several other agents piled into cars.

"That's Blaine's address," Roanne said breathlessly, even as she groped for her seat belt.

"Not a shock. Amateurs who play with explosives frequently blow themselves up by accident."

"Do you think that's what happened? Or did he blow up his house or garage and hope we'd assume he was inside?"

"Don't know. But after seeing that look on his face..."

Nolan was driving fast. Too fast. She clutched the seat belt with both hands but didn't argue.

He didn't need to recall the route; black smoke roiled

in a huge plume above the disaster, giving away their destination.

Several fire trucks from different stations had beaten them there. Some directed streams of water at neighboring houses to wet down flying cinders, while others were aimed into the blast zone. Roanne wasn't surprised to see that the inferno was centered on a crater dug by the force of the explosion. Blaine's garage, of course. His house was damaged but still stood. A tan van had been tossed onto its side into the middle of the street. Even the metal was singed and mangled.

Staring but not yet getting out, Nolan said harshly, "That gutless wonder chose this instead of joining Fedor in prison. He didn't care if he brought down the neighbors' homes, maybe killed a few more people."

"He never cared about that."

"No." Nolan let out a long breath. "I'm not sure how close we can get, but let's take a look."

She nodded, exited the vehicle, then stopped dead. Was that...an *arm*? In a shirt she recognized? Her swept gaze found other body parts.

Blaine Weightman *definitely* was dead, and in a way that struck her as poetic justice. Which didn't prevent her from turning away and dry heaving.

SEVERAL HOURS LATER, Nolan had coaxed Roanne into a corner booth at a local café where they'd eaten before. She was holding herself together, but any color had been bleached from her face, and he hated seeing the turmoil in her eyes. He felt sick to his stomach, too, but not because of the human remnants left in the bomb crater. He'd seen worse, occasionally the horrific deaths of people he'd known, even called friends.

No, he felt sick to his stomach for another reason. Maybe he should wait before he raised the subject; he fully intended to spend the night with her if she was willing. It was the future he wanted to talk about, even knowing the discussion probably was premature.

It just didn't feel that way to him.

Neither of them even glanced at the menu. Roanne asked only for a bowl of soup after saying she hoped it would warm her and stop the shakes. As soon as the waitress left them, he reached across the table and waited for her to put her hand in his.

"You okay?"

She made a pathetic attempt at smiling. "Fine. More or less. Just..."

"You haven't seen anything like that before."

"I saw a few firefighters who are going to have nightmares, but the ATF agents took it in stride. You, too."

"They have a similar background to mine. I joined the EOD—Explosive Ordnance Disposal team—after an IED blew a jeep apart right in front of me." His throat worked. "I thought I could protect more troops by preventing those attacks than by fighting."

She nodded, her gaze glued to him. After a moment, she asked, "You'll be heading back to Seattle."

"There's enough to tie up that it'll probably be a couple of days. I want to talk to you—"

The waitress appeared with their meals. He nodded and thanked her, while Roanne remained mute.

With them alone again, she only waited.

"Are you tied to Rosendaal forever because of your father?"

She blinked a few times. "No. Of course not. I think he really needed me at first, and he loves having me close by. But he keeps talking about me, you know, having my own family." By this time, her cheeks were pink. "I mean, if I move away, he could follow me, but honestly, I don't think he would. He has tons of friends here."

"I have to stay in Seattle," he said hoarsely, "because of the job."

Roanne nodded.

He couldn't remember the last time *he'd* blinked. His eyes burned. Neither of them had so much as shaken out a napkin onto their lap.

"This may be too soon for you." Of course it was. "But I'm in love with you," he concluded. "We don't live so far apart that we can't date or spend an occasional night together, but I know what I want."

Her lips had parted. She dampened them with the tip of her tongue. "You mean that," she whispered.

"I do. I've never felt anything like this before. Today—" Nolan's shoulders moved. "It was agony."

"I…felt the same. Knowing what you were having to do. If you'd made the tiniest misstep, you'd have been the first one to die."

"I can't say the thought didn't cross my mind, but mostly I thought about you and all those kids."

"I kept thinking that in talking them into enrolling, I may have been responsible for killing them."

His hand tightened on hers. "You know that's not true. You did the right thing. Having someone with more than a few screws loose isn't something any of us can predict or blame ourselves for."

"You're right. I know that."

Nolan was suffering. What if she'd steered the conversation back to Weightman because she didn't know what to say to him—or wasn't eager to let him down?

Could he find a hotel room for tonight if she said *I'm sorry, but no*?

Her fingers curled around his. "I think I may have fallen in love with you that night in the hospital. And since then, you've never, oh, belittled me because I'm a woman in law enforcement or not listened. You've even acted on my ideas. Do you know how rare that is?"

"No." He barely got the word out. "That's because you're smart and knowledgeable. I'd have been a fool *not* to listen to you."

A smile trembled on her lips. "I can give notice as soon as we're sure we're ready. And well, I'll have to put my house on the market."

"As far as I'm concerned, the sooner the better. In the meantime…do you have any vacation time coming?"

"Yes, something like ten days."

"Why don't we spend it together? Hawaii, New York City, any place you want."

"If it's with you, I don't care where we go." Then Roanne's lips curved, just a little. "Although it would be nice if we could find someplace with no cell phone service."

"That sounds good to me, too." Nolan glanced down at his untouched food. "I still have to do my job this afternoon, but all I'll be thinking about spending the night with you."

"I can hardly wait." Her smile was the most beautiful he'd ever seen. "For all of it."

* * * * *

Get up to 4 Free Books!

We'll send you 2 free books from each series you try PLUS a free Mystery Gift.

FREE Value Over $25

Both the **Harlequin Intrigue®** and **Harlequin® Romantic Suspense** series feature compelling novels filled with heart-racing action-packed romance that will keep you on the edge of your seat.

YES! Please send me 2 FREE novels from the Harlequin Intrigue or Harlequin Romantic Suspense series and my FREE gift (gift is worth about $10 retail). After receiving them, if I don't wish to receive any more books, I can return the shipping statement marked "cancel." If I don't cancel, I will receive 6 brand-new Harlequin Intrigue Larger-Print books every month and be billed just $7.19 each in the U.S. or $7.99 each in Canada, or 4 brand-new Harlequin Romantic Suspense books every month and be billed just $6.39 each in the U.S. or $7.19 each in Canada, a savings of 20% off the cover price. It's quite a bargain! Shipping and handling is just 50¢ per book in the U.S. and $1.25 per book in Canada.* I understand that accepting the 2 free books and gift places me under no obligation to buy anything. I can always return a shipment and cancel at any time by calling the number below. The free books and gift are mine to keep no matter what I decide.

Choose one:
- ☐ **Harlequin Intrigue Larger-Print** (199/399 BPA G36Y)
- ☐ **Harlequin Romantic Suspense** (240/340 BPA G36Y)
- ☐ **Or Try Both!** (199/399 & 240/340 BPA G36Z)

Name (please print)

Address _____ Apt. #

City _____ State/Province _____ Zip/Postal Code

Email: Please check this box ☐ if you would like to receive newsletters and promotional emails from Harlequin Enterprises ULC and its affiliates. You can unsubscribe anytime.

Mail to the **Harlequin Reader Service:**
IN U.S.A.: P.O. Box 1341, Buffalo, NY 14240-8531
IN CANADA: P.O. Box 603, Fort Erie, Ontario L2A 5X3

Want to explore our other series or interested in ebooks? Visit www.ReaderService.com or call 1-800-873-8635.

---

*Terms and prices subject to change without notice. Prices do not include sales taxes, which will be charged (if applicable) based on your state or country of residence. Canadian residents will be charged applicable taxes. Offer not valid in Quebec. This offer is limited to one order per household. Books received may not be as shown. Not valid for current subscribers to the Harlequin Intrigue or Harlequin Romantic Suspense series. All orders subject to approval. Credit or debit balances in a customer's account(s) may be offset by any other outstanding balance owed by or to the customer. Please allow 4 to 6 weeks for delivery. Offer available while quantities last.

Your Privacy—Your information is being collected by Harlequin Enterprises ULC, operating as Harlequin Reader Service. For a complete summary of the information we collect, how we use this information and to whom it is disclosed, please visit our privacy notice located at https://corporate.harlequin.com/privacy-notice. Notice to California Residents – Under California law, you have specific rights to control and access your data. For more information on these rights and how to exercise them, visit https://corporate.harlequin.com/california-privacy. For additional information for residents of other U.S. states that provide their residents with certain rights with respect to personal data, visit https://corporate.harlequin.com/other-state-residents-privacy-rights/.

HIHRS25